MW01146657

Trai

A M/M BDSM Straight To Gay First Time Erotic Romance
By Charlotte Storm

Summary

After graduating college, Aiden Montgomery isn't sure what he's going to do with his life, other than marry the woman his parents told him he had to. Then, his friend offers to get him a job working for his father.

It's a dream job, dream hours, and decent pay. Yes, his friend's only offering to help because he's gay and has a thing for Aiden, but Aiden's straight. So turning him down shouldn't be an issue. That is, until Aiden meets his new boss, Griffin Hart.

Griffin is everything Aiden secretly fantasizes about. Secret, because no one can know he longs to submit to a man who can take control, who can take Aiden across a threshold he so desperately wants to crawl across on hands and knees.

Aiden soon finds out Griffin is exactly the kind of man who can take him from straight to gay, push his boundaries and buttons in a way he never dreamed possible. But Aiden's boundaries are there for a reason. He's engaged to a woman his strict, abusive family picked out for him. And his boss's son isn't too happy about Aiden falling for another man, even if that man is his father.

When their relationship is revealed, everything they've worked for threatened, Aiden will have to decide if he'll succumb to the pressure from his family and deny who he's always been, or if he'll be the man he's been *trained* to be.

Trained By The Boss is a *M/M BDSM straight to gay first time erotic romance* intended for an adult audience.

Copyright © 2018, Charlotte Storm. All rights reserved.

No part of this publication may be reproduced in any form or by any electronic or mechanical means, including information storage and retrieval systems, without written permission from the author, except for the use of brief quotations in a book review.

This is a work of fiction. Names, characters, places, and incidents are the product of the author's imagination, or are used fictitiously. Any resemblance to actual persons or events is purely coincidental.

Author's Note: Yes, this book was originally released by Charlotte Storm & CC Wylde. Don't worry. I didn't just remove CC Wylde's name. They're both me. I'm consolidating pen names. Thank you for understanding :-)

• • • •

JOIN **Charlotte Storm**'s VIP mailing list to get an **exclusive M/F BDSM download**, and all the latest news about new releases, giveaways, and freebies!

https://www.subscribepage.com/CharlotteStorm

Find all of her books here:

https://www.amazon.com/Charlotte-Storm/e/
B07B7QMR4G

Listen to all of her audio books here:

https://www.audible.com/author/Charlotte-Storm/
B07B7QMR4G

Dedication

To love, in all its forms . . .

Chapter 1

My feet are sore, and the butterflies in my stomach have long since died by the time I walk across the stage and accept my diploma. No faster way to kill the excited buzz of finally graduating college than by making you wait for hours, in the hot sun, for five seconds of fame.

Thank God for post-graduation parties.

And Geo Hart throws the best kind of parties.

After taking countless pictures with my parents, I ditch my cap and gown for something a little more stylish and formal, and head to Geo's house, a sprawling estate in the hills of Rancho Santa Fe, located in sunny San Diego.

Geo has money. Or rather, his father has money. CEO of a local business solutions firm, Griffin Hart has made quite a name for himself in the community, and among recent business grads like myself. Landing a coveted internship at his company is almost a guaranteed career boost.

It's why I agreed to meet Geo early, get to his house before the party starts. He wants to introduce me to his father, give me an advantage over other applicants. I appreciate it, I do. But with Geo, there are always strings attached. And I don't like the strings Geo's pulling.

He's had a crush on me for almost the entire year we've been friends. I have zero issues with Geo being gay. He has lots of issues with me telling him I'm not. I know accepting his offer to meet his dad is me taking advantage of him, pimping myself out to get ahead. But I just can't bring myself to push him away.

I need this internship, need to show my family that putting me through college wasn't a waste of their money. Besides, even if I *did* want to screw around with Geo, which I don't, I couldn't. My family has strict ideals about how I should live my life. Hell, they even have my future fiancé all picked out for me. Lily, a girl I grew up with, now all woman. My family has been doing more than hinting she's the perfect choice to be my wife ever since I graduated high school.

It's nice, I guess, to have my future so completely mapped out. Other people I know have no clue what they want to do. Who they want to be. They don't have a family to tell them how to live their lives. I can appreciate that my parents care for me, want what they think is best.

Sometimes, it feels good to know I'm supported. But most of the time, I want to rage against the bars around my life suffocating the real me I can never admit exists.

"Want a drink?" Geo asks when he answers the door. "You look like you could use a fucking drink, Aiden."

Geo grabs me by the arm and drags me inside. It takes me a minute to get over the shock of how nice his house is. Marble, granite, oak, artwork...basically anything you'd see inside a modern living magazine.

Leading me through the open floor space—where rooms are connected by arches, and just about every room on this level is visible from anywhere else—Geo leads me to the back patio area. I don't fight him, or make him let go of my bicep, which he strokes lazily with his thumb. No, I just go with the flow, and ignore the pulse of excitement that shoots down my spine, pooling in my dick, with the idea of being dragged around, told what to do.

That fire quickly douses when I remind myself that it's Geo doing the leading. There's nothing inherently wrong with him. He's good looking, if tattooed bratty bad boys with long black hair and piercings are your thing. He just isn't my type, isn't what I imagine when I fantasize about being with a man.

Fuck! No, he isn't my type because he has the *wrong* equipment. He isn't my type because I like women. Because Montgomery men aren't *fags*.

I scrub a hand over my face to dislodge my father's voice from my mind, and plop down in the chair Geo puts me in.

"You want a beer?" Geo reaches into a cooler. "Or something stronger?" He shuts the cooler lid, taps on his lip ring, then grins in the wicked way only Geo can. The way that tells me he's up to zero good. "Something stronger, I think."

"Geo, you know I don't really drink." *With you*. I leave out that part because Geo's doing me a solid with his dad, and there's no reason to dredge up the past.

Geo licks his lips, his eyes doing that thing where I feel like I might as well be naked. "I distinctly remember you getting drunk not that long ago."

I roll my eyes, trying to play off my discomfort. "That was once. I learned my lesson. No more tequila in my life."

Ever.

"Besides," I press on, hoping he'll drop it, "I'm about to meet your dad. Do you really think he'll want to hire me if I'm drunk before my interview?"

"You're such a prude, Montgomery," he teases, but thankfully doesn't put to use the bar already set up for the party.

"And you're a slut, Hart," I tease right back, because we're friends, and it's true.

Geo smiles like he just heard the funniest joke and he's trying not to laugh. I don't get what's so funny. I've called him a slut plenty before. Hell, *he's* called *himself* a slut more than anyone has.

The sound of a throat clearing behind me makes me want to throw myself off the balcony. Makes me wish I'd taken that drink.

"Aiden Montgomery, I presume?"

Still facing Geo, I close my eyes and will the heat riding my nerves to chill the hell out. Not only did I just call my hopefully future boss's son a slut, I can't stop my dick from thickening inside my pants at the sound of his voice.

Strong. Deep. Bold. Everything a man's voice should be. The type of tone and timbre I dream about when I imagine being bound, gagged, and *forced* to do unspeakable things. Immoral things. Unacceptable things.

Say something! The voice inside my head screams. Mimicking his earlier action, I clear my throat. But what comes out of my mouth is nowhere near as sexy.

"Y-Yeah...um, yes. I'm Aiden."

When I turn to face him, all the air rushes out of my lungs, like someone just sucker punched me in the gut. Holy *fuck*. I've never met Griffin Hart in person, just seen pictures of him in articles I've read.

None of those pictures do justice in capturing his true presence. The magnetism radiating off of him strong enough to shred the metal cage around my life, keeping me on the straight and narrow.

His short, gray hair is impeccably styled. Instead of shaving close to the skin, he wears a five o'clock shadow which makes the sharp angles of his face more severe, not less. More hand-somely breathtaking. His vest-jacket-pant combo is precision tailored to every line of his fit, muscular body. And even though he's only a few inches taller than me, I feel miniscule next to him.

No, not miniscule. Submissive. It's all I can do not to drop to my knees and beg him to put a collar on me. But I don't think that's the best way to get a job, or make a first impression.

"I'm Griffin Hart." He reaches out his hand.

Before I take it, I wipe my palm on my pants, way too close to my crotch. He notices. Something about the way he looks tells me he notices everything, including the erection that's impossible to hide.

Instead of dying from embarrassment like I want to, I take his hand, relish in the feel of his skin on mine, and shit. I should not be having these thoughts about him. About any man. "Nice to meet you," I somehow manage to say.

Gripping my hand harder, Griffin pulls me close, until his face is inches from mine. His hot breath fans my face when he says, "*Sir*. It's nice to meet you, *sir*."

I lick my lips, stare at his. "I'm sorry. S-Sir."

He lets go of my hand, puts much needed distance between us, even if I don't want the distance. I want closer, and that, more than anything, is the most dangerous thought I've had to-day.

"Dad, don't be a hardass," Geo says from somewhere over my shoulder.

Something flashes behind Griffin's eyes, and his lips twitch in an almost smile. I swear he knows that I want him to be a hardass. To be so much more.

"Join me in my office, Aiden. We'll get the interview started, as I'm sure you'll want to party with your friends when we're finished."

Following behind him like a good little subordinate, I risk a glance behind me at Geo. For what reason? I don't know. Maybe to see if he notices how flustered his father makes me? For moral support?

The last is laughable. Nothing about Geo is moral.

He gives me a thumbs up and a wicked grin. Classic Geo.

Griffin leads me through an open walkway, then down a staircase, to an alcove with a detached office. "I covet my privacy, Mr. Montgomery," he says when I ask why his office is separate from the rest of the house, and why there's a bathroom attached. "Are you good at keeping secrets?"

His hard, dark eyes stare into me, needle prick on skin type feel. I shift on my feet, try and suppress the notion that I have anything to hide.

"I don't have any secrets, Mr. Hart. Sir," I quickly add when his lips pinch into a thin line.

Now they curve up. My heart jumps in my chest because I made him happy. Why I should care so much about how I make him feel, I don't want to look at too closely. Unless it has to do with an internship, and my future.

"Everyone has secrets," he says as he sits in his chair. It's a leather wingback with polished wooden armrests.

I take the much less impressive chair across from him. At least, I'm about to when he says, "I haven't told you to sit, Mr. Montgomery."

Straightening up, I eye the chair, then him. "I'm sorry, I just thought—"

"I'm sorry, *sir*," he cuts me off, correcting me.

"What?" I ask, not exactly sure what he means.

"When you've done something wrong, you apologize, and end with sir. Always end with sir. I don't give a shit about your excuses. I just want your compliance. Understand?"

He steeples his fingers underneath his chin and waits for my answer.

Shame burns the underside of my skin at the verbal spanking I just got from Geo's father. But that isn't what heats my blood and sends it surging south.

"May I sit?" I ask in my best mannered tone. "Sir," I add, and damn. How can one word make me so fucking hard?

"Not until you answer my question." His eyes roam over my clothes, my hair, my face, my shoes. He's studying me, and even though I graduated Magna Cum Laude, this seems like a test I'm failing. Miserably.

"What question, sir?"

He leans forward in his chair, his gaze fixed thoroughly on my thick erection.

Shit. There's no way I'm getting an internship.

"Can you keep a secret? In my line of work, insider knowledge and intellectual property are hot commodities. Being discreet is very important."

I swallow hard, praying for a drop of moisture to enter my mouth, make my voice smoother and steadier than I feel.

"Yes. Mr. Hart. *Sir*. I'm very good at keeping secrets. At being discreet."

This time, it's just shame that burns me. If my father could see into my head right now, he'd disown me. My mother, too.

Because of them, I've gotten good at burying things in deep, dark holes.

"You aren't being discreet now." He gestures to my crotch. "Do you want to explain yourself, Mr. Montgomery?"

No. I don't have anything to say, because what the hell could I possibly? My dick is hard because I've always wanted a man to take control of me, but have been too closeted my entire life to admit it? That I've never been turned on by anyone as much as him, not even when watching gay porn that one time I got drunk with his son? Not when his son kissed me, and I let him?

This was a mistake. I should've never taken advantage of Geo's offer. Karma has a way of biting people in the ass, the universe a way of righting wrongs.

This is wrong. Me wanting him. Me being here, hard, and so fucking turned on I can't breathe. Or maybe it's the cage around my life that keeps me from breathing.

"I'm sorry to have wasted your time, Mr. Hart. Sir." I turn my back on him and adjust my crotch, then head for the door, hoping I can sneak out of the house without Geo noticing.

Before I can open the office door, Mr. Hart's voice freezes me in place.

"Stop, Aiden."

Two words. Two fucking words that have all the power in the world.

I do what he says, because I want to. A part of me *needs* to.

"Turn around." He's behind me, no longer sitting in his chair.

The way the hairs on the back of my neck stand on end, I know he's close. When I obey, and face him, I realize I was right. He's close. Too close. Heat radiates off him. It beats against me, burns me, like being too long in the sun.

I can't catch an even breath. When I do manage to breathe in, the scent of him coats my tongue, slides down my throat, nestles in my lungs. He's inside me, and the only thing we've done is shake hands.

"I didn't tell you that you could leave." His voice is hard, cold, even if his eyes express sympathy. For what? I couldn't say.

"I'm sorry, sir." My voice barely travels across the space between our bodies. There isn't much. "I just thought—"

Griffin cages me between his arms, putting them on the wall on either side of my head. "No excuses, Aiden. I've told you once. I won't warn you again. If I want your opinion on something, I'll ask. Any other response you give will be either an affirmative or a negative, followed by sir."

"Yes, sir," I say, fighting the urge to touch my cock, to find some kind of relief. It's painful, how hard I am. How hard this man makes me.

"Good."

Griffin drops his arms and steps back. He juts his chin at my bulge, and I swear I see amusement in his eyes. Maybe even hunger.

"You'll never have to be ashamed of who you are around me, Mr. Montgomery. I don't care *who* or *what* you prefer, as long as it's legal, and you're honest with me."

"Do-Does that mean I got the internship?" I ask, then add, "Sir?"

"No." He turns his back to me, goes to his chair, sits down, and starts typing away on his keyboard.

"No?" I ask, more confused about his answer than my sexuality. "I don't understand."

"I'm not giving you the internship, Mr. Montgomery. You're overqualified, easily trainable, and eager to learn." I could swear he also mutters something like, "Eager to please me."

"Um, okay. So, I don't have the internship?" I knew it was too much to hope for, but I really needed this for my family. For me.

"No."

"So, am I excused then, sir?"

"Yes," he says, not bothering to glance my way from whatever's on his screen. "See you Monday morning, eight o'clock sharp. Give the receptionist your name when you arrive. I'll leave instructions for you."

I know I'm standing here like an idiot, but either I have extreme short-term memory loss, or I missed something during our conversation. Playing it over in my head, I can't come up with anything that helps me understand if I got the internship or not.

Just as my mouth pops open to ask him another question, Griffin tears his gaze from the computer and locks it on me. "I'm not hiring you for the internship. I want you as my personal assistant. Mine quit recently. I need a new one. I'm giving you a job, a real job, if you want it."

"Oh? Yeah. Yes! Uh, yes, sir. I want the job."

"Good. Then I'll see you at eight. Now, go. Enjoy the party." His eyes skim down my chest, over my stomach, and land on my still hard cock. "Find some relief. I'm sure my son, Geo, can help you with that."

My heart leaps in my chest, tries to claw its way up my throat. "What?" I croak, the word flying out of my mouth before I can stop it? "I'm not...we've never...that's not...I'm *straight*."

Mr. Hart cocks an eyebrow. "Really? I just assumed..." He leaves the rest unspoken as he continues to stare at my crotch. "Geo tends to have good taste. And the way he spoke about you made me think you two were lovers."

Lovers. Something twists in my gut at that word. But not because of Geo.

"No." I shake my head, maybe a bit too hard. "We aren't lovers. Never have been. Never will be. Just friends." The kiss between us doesn't count.

A thought occurs to me, and I bite my lip. "So, do you still want to hire me now you know I'm not with your son? Sir?"

Mr. Hart's smile is genuine, lights up his whole face, making him more handsome than he has any damn right being.

"Actually, Mr. Montgomery, it makes me want you more." With a final once-over, Griffin shifts his attention back to his computer. "See you Monday. Enjoy the party."

Chapter 2

Monday rolls around at break-neck speed.

I'm almost late because I can't figure out what to wear, or get my hair to cooperate. I settle for business casual: button shirt, tie, and the only pair of charcoal gray slacks that I've had tailored to fit.

Thankfully, I'm not late, unless someone considers showing up one minute ahead of schedule, late.

"Welcome to Griffin Business Solutions," the receptionist says in the kind of cheery voice every Monday-morning hater must resent. "You're Aiden Montgomery. Correct?"

"Yeah." I hold out my hand for her to shake.

She stares at it, reaches for something underneath the desk, then straightens. Into my palm she places a large yellow envelope.

"There you go," she says, her smile about as real as her veneers. "Good luck, Mr. Montgomery."

"Good luck?" I stare at the envelope, half expecting it to explode or something. "Why? Am I going to need it?"

Her smile fades, her lips pressing together into a thin line. "Probably," she says in a moment of honesty, her facade cast aside faster than the next fad on social media. "Mr. Hart has *particular* tastes and expectations. Meet or exceed them, I'm sure you'll do fine. Anything less than excellence, and..." She points to the front doors I just walked through. "You get the rest, right?"

Particular tastes and expectations? What the hell does that mean?

"Right. Thanks for the heads-up."

The phone rings. She answers, ignoring me. Guess that's my cue.

Stepping to the side of the reception desk, I tear open the envelope. Inside is a cell phone and nothing else. Bringing the screen to life, I notice there are several text messages from a number programmed with the name *Sir*. A thrill flashes through my bloodstream, my thoughts immediately going to my interview with Mr. Hart.

Discarding the envelope in a nearby trash can, I tap on the messages and read them, rapid succession. Each one details a specific erand, time, and location. I glance at the current time and notice that, if I don't move my ass five minutes ago, I'll be late for the first assignment.

Cursing under my breath, I get back into my car and get to work.

It's lunch hour by the time I make it to Mr. Hart's house. My stomach growls in discontent at being empty, my reserves made low by rushing around all morning.

Letting myself into his private office, I hang his dry cleaning on a hook by the door then wait, expecting any moment for Griffin Hart to greet me.

After ten minutes, I suspect he isn't here, though where he is, I don't know. And I can't figure out why he'd ask me to come to his home office instead of his business office.

After another minute or so, my curiosity gets the better of me. I start to nose around his desk to see if he left further instructions. Sure enough, on his desk is a note.

Mr. Montgomery,

If you're reading this, I trust you completed my errands in a timely manner. You will sit in the chair by the sliding door to the patio, hands palms up on your thighs, and wait for me.

Don't disappoint.

~S

I read the note a few more times to make sure it's real, that this isn't some joke. Palms up? Is he serious? I mean, how would he even know? And, S? Who the hell is S?

The phone in my pocket buzzes. I pull it out, glance at the screen. Text from Sir.

Oh. My. Fucking. *God*! S equals Sir.

A bolder, more comfortable-in-their-own-skin type of person would admit how fucking hot and turned on they are. I'm not that person. Instead, I adjust my crotch and read the text.

Sir: *You aren't sitting down.*

Sir: *Do what you're told. Now.*

My eyes widen as I read the text messages, then scan the office. Shit. He can *see* me. But how?

Cramming the phone back into my pocket, I walk across the large office to the sliding glass door that opens to a patio. Next to it is a simple, wooden chair. Plain, but sturdy.

I sit down, rub my palms against my slacks, then remember I'm supposed to place them up. I do as instructed. The phone inside my pocket does not buzz again.

I lose track of time after the first ten or so minutes. The sun coming through the window is hot on my thighs, my up-turned palms, but I don't dare move. Not even to wipe the drip of sweat off my forehead, or relieve my aching shoulders, tight from tension.

No. Not tension. Anticipation.

After what feels like forever, the knob on the office door turns slowly, and the presence that is Griffin Hart steps inside.

I wince at how fucking striking he looks in his blue tailored suit, then divert my eyes out the window so he can't see the effect he has on me.

It's wrong, this effect. He's my boss. I'm straight. Definitely not gay, despite not having many girlfriends. I guess I always wondered what the point was because my parents had already picked out my future wife.

Now, I'm not so sure that was the reason. Doesn't matter. I need this job, need my family's approval and financial support. Living in California is cost prohibitive for a recent college grad. Hell, most people, actually.

"Mr. Montgomery?" Griffin's voice brings me back from my mental ledge. "Did you hear what I said?"

Licking my lips, I stare into his face. "I'm sorry, sir. I didn't."

"Everything okay?" he asks, his brow crinkling with concern.

"Honestly?" I say before I have the chance to fully think it through.

Griffin's dark eyes harden. The muscles along the edge of his jaw ripple and writhe. "Always honesty, Aiden."

I think I might be into you, which terrifies me because I can't be gay. I just can't. I'll lose my family, my friends...my entire life will be gone. A gilded cage is better than having nowhere to live.

"I'm cramping, and my back hurts from sitting in one position for so long."

Griffin breathes a sigh of relief, and I can't begin to imagine what that was for.

"Stand," he says simply. I obey, and *God*. Being under his control is the easiest thing in the world.

"Turn around."

When I do, his hands go to my shoulders. His strong fingers work out the knots below my shoulder blades and along my neck to the back of my skull.

My brain tells me it should feel weird, him touching me, massaging me, his hands on my body. My body doesn't seem to mind at all. In fact, it wants more of him touching me, against me, working out all of my kinks.

"Is this okay?" he asks as he glides his hand up the back of my neck.

A moan escapes my mouth, and I huff out a huge breath, which makes me relax even more. "Yes." The word leaves my lips without my brain's permission, but I can't give a fuck about that right now.

His grip on my neck tightens, his entire body presses against my back. He leans in close, his lips grazing my earlobe. That one movement ratchets back up my tension, but in a good way.

"Yes, what?" His tone is little more than a growl. My dick is little less than fully hard.

"Yes, sir." The words tumble from my lips as if giving myself over to him completely would be simple. Easy. It would also ruin me.

Having lost control over my body from the moment he walked into the room, I press my hips back, my ass sliding along his hard front.

His hard front. Holy *shit*.

Mr. Hart's grip on my neck tightens even more. His other hand goes to my hip. He squeezes, causing me to gasp, before pushing me away and stepping back.

"I trust you got everything done that I asked," he says, voice calm, as if he's unaffected by what just happened.

I don't understand how that can be true. I'm painfully affected, the evidence leaving no room for negotiation in my slacks. Taking a few calming breaths, I beg my body to chill. To relax. To not be so damn hard.

It doesn't work.

Instead of facing him, I stare out the sliding glass door to the garden beyond. "Y-yeah. Yes, sir. I did."

He points to the chair. I catch the motion in my periphery. "And it's obvious to me you can follow directions. Do what you're told."

"I can, sir." I want to do so much more.

"Do you like being told what to do? Like giving up control?"

Closing my eyes, I swallow hard. My mouth is dry, so it's difficult to speak. I do it anyway, because he asked me a question, and I don't want to disappoint him.

"I do, sir."

His office chair creaks, signaling that he's sitting at his computer. "Why?"

"Makes things easier, sir."

A chuckle rumbles his chest. "What things?"

"Everything," I answer, because it's the best, most honest answer I have.

Mr. Hart remains quiet for a long time. I'm tempted to turn around, but he didn't tell me to, and I'm still hard enough it's best if I don't.

"You're dismissed, Mr. Montgomery," he finally says. "You did well for your first day."

"Thank you, sir." I head for the door, not once looking at my boss.

"See you tomorrow at eight sharp," he says.

I nod, then get out of there as fast as I can.

Chapter 3

The next few weeks fly by.

Mr. Hart keeps me busy running errands, following him around the office to learn the business, and taking copious amount of notes. My wrists and fingers cramp after the third day, so I make sure to stretch, and make good use of the company gym after hours.

I've never really been a huge gym buff. Preferred to play team sports and jog instead. But with how hard Mr. Hart has me running, keeping in shape is a must.

My work phone buzzes. I can't help the thrill that spikes through me when I see who it is.

He has to know what he does to me. And I'm pretty sure him programming his title into the phone is the proof.

Sir: *Meet me at my house in an hour. Wear workout clothes and running shoes.*

I stop by my house to change my clothes, which takes longer than it should because I'm torn between looking good for him and wearing something comfortable. I have no idea what he has planned, but I have to imagine it's workout related.

I'm halfway out the door when my father stops me. "Aiden. Where are you off to in such a hurry?"

"Sorry, Dad. No time to talk. Gotta get back to work." I palm my keys, try and close the door.

He puts his foot in the way, blocking it. "You look like a slob, Aiden. Don't forget how lucky you are to have gotten this job. The real test of what kind of man you are is if you can keep it."

My gut drops to my shoes, not only because of how small I feel underneath my father's microscope, but also because, if I don't move my ass, I'm going to be late.

"I know, Dad. Mr. Hart asked me to change clothes."

The judgmental eyebrow I know all too well encroaches on his hairline. "That's a strange request."

He has no idea, this is one of the *least* strange things Griffin has asked of me.

"Not really. It's my job to go where he goes, be available to him for anything." A thrilling tingle followed by heated shame burns through my bloodstream at the thought of being available to do *anything* for Mr. Hart. "I'm probably just going to be taking notes while he works out."

I pull out the phone, check the time. "Sorry, Dad. I really have to go."

"I've invited Lily and her parents over for dinner tonight. I expect you to be home by six so you can greet them when they arrive. I expect you and Lily will be spending more time together now that you've graduated college, with her only a semester behind you."

"Lily?" Her name leaves my mouth like a curse word. It isn't her fault. She's nice enough. Pretty. Kind. Everything my parents want for me. She just isn't something I want for myself.

"Yes. Lily. Your future fiancé." My father's eyes harden, issuing the challenge and the threat of what comes after if I refuse, argue, or basically want to be my own person.

I should tell him to fuck off. That this is my life. I'll do with it what I want. I'll do *who* I want.

"S-Sure. Six it is. Sounds good."

I'm a damn coward, but I'm also going to be a late coward. I don't know why, but something tells me I don't want to find out what happens if I displease Mr. Hart.

I know I'm in trouble the moment I arrive. Not only am I fifteen minutes late, Mr. Hart is standing in the middle of his office, foot tapping an impatient rhythm. His arms are crossed over his toned chest, visible through his lycra tee. His biceps bulge from the strain hardening every muscle from neck to calf.

The source of the strain has to be me. Has to be that I'm late. I open my mouth to make an excuse, to tell him that it was my father's fault, not mine. But Mr. Hart doesn't want my excuses. He's made that clear already. It would only piss him off further if I went down that path.

Lowering my head in what I hope is a submissive gesture, I put my hands behind my back and hunch my shoulders. "Sorry I'm late, sir."

"You know how much it displeases me when you don't follow directions, don't you, Mr. Montgomery?" His tone is harsh. Strict. But he isn't cruel, and he doesn't even sound angry. He sounds...almost happy. Has he been waiting for me to screw up? And now that I finally have, he can punish me?

Fuck. A part of me wishes he would. Punish me. Control me. Force me over the straight line I keep dancing around.

"I do, sir."

"You've excelled at following directions for weeks. It's disappointing..."

I expect him to say that he's disappointed I let him down. I failed in some way. That I'm not good enough for this job.

"...that you've waited so long."

"What?" My head pops up, my eyes searching his. That was not what I expected.

I also don't expect for him to be so fucking ravenous. The look on his face. *Jesus.*

That's when I feel it. The pieces inside me that are too rigid, snap. Break. Fall apart. Fall away, until it's just me and a man that makes me want to admit the truth I've denied my whole life.

My dick instantly thickens. My lungs struggle to take in air. I suppress the urge to whimper. To cower. To get on my knees in front of him and beg him to own me in any way he wants to. Every way. Not just my job, career, and future. But my body.

Griffin approaches me in the slow way a jungle cat stalks prey. "Do you remember when you said giving up control makes everything easier?" he asks, his voice taking on a deep quality that has my nerve endings firing in rapid succession.

I nod. "Yes, sir."

"I've been thinking about that statement for weeks. About what it could mean for you. For...*us*."

I don't dare speak. Dare breathe. I can't say it, because I don't have the balls, and I'm not sure I'm ready to make the leap. But if he gets there on his own, I won't stop him. Won't deny it.

"You know what I think, Mr. Montgomery?"

"No, sir."

"I think you want me to take control. *Full* control. Because you don't have any. Not at home. Not at your job. And not with this."

Crowding my body with his, Griffin presses his chest against mine, our thighs touching. He forces my knees apart with his leg, wraps his hand around the steel rod in my shorts.

I unravel.

One goddamn touch destroys me completely. I should be ashamed of the noise that works its way up my throat, out of my mouth. But the sensation of him touching me is too good.

Something that feels this amazing isn't wrong. Right?

"You're safe with me, Aiden. You can let go." Griffin's words are little more than a whisper, but they resonate loud enough to crumble my walls.

Snaking my hands across his chest to his shoulders, I hold on, dig my fingers into his muscles, as I relish in the feel of his hand on me.

"Do you want to belong to me, Aiden?" he asks as he strokes slowly down my shaft, his breath heating the space between our lips. "Think before you answer, and know that any answer you give is acceptable. I don't want you to think that your job"—he pinches the head of my cock through my shorts—"depends on this. It doesn't."

My fingers dig harder into his shoulder muscles. My hips buck forward, begging him to go further. Fuck, I want him, want *this*, more than I've ever wanted anything.

"I want to be yours completely, sir," I say on an exhalation, my body, my bones, my soul releasing with the air.

"I'm happy to hear that, Aiden. Now, do you think I should punish you for being late?"

"Yes. Please, sir. Please punish me."

"Oh, I plan to." Griffin chuckles, mocking me. "I wonder, do you still think you're straight?"

The answer catches in my throat. His grip on my cock tightens, almost to the point of pain. I grit my teeth, give him the most honest answer I can. "I do-don't know, sir."

Pulling back, Mr. Hart locks eyes with mine. What he sees, I can't imagine. But I know what I see. What I want.

When he presses forward, closes the distance between us, I catch his mouth with mine, eager to taste him. Eager to please him.

When his tongue presses against my lips, I let him in. Right now, there isn't anything of his I wouldn't let in, anywhere he pressed.

Grabbing the back of my neck, he deepens the kiss, claiming my mouth with his. He growls. I catch the sound, drink it down. Take it into me.

Just as quickly as he started, he stops. "Now do you know?" he asks, staring at my lips.

They're swollen, rubbed raw from the prickles of his facial hair. It's a sensation I never thought I'd feel. One I never want to live without.

"I'm starting to, sir."

"Good." When he lets go of me, I want to scream at him to put his hands back on me. Jack me off, let me finish. Claim my mouth, and after, my body. "Ready to go for a run?" he asks as if the past five minutes never happened?

"What?" I stare at him, then at the bulge in my shorts. "W-What about this? What about me being yours?"

"You are mine." He turns his back on me, heads to the office door.

I lick my lips, not sure how hard I can press, and definitely not sure what the hell is going on. "But I thought...I mean, I want to be yours *now*, sir."

Griffin stops mid-stride. His fists clench and unclench, and he rolls his head around on his shoulders like he's working out his muscles.

"You *are* mine now." When he turns to face me, his jaw is hard set. His fierce gaze even harder. "Right now. And on this run. And for as long as we both agree. *Only* mine, Aiden. Do you understand?"

"Of course, only yours, sir. I don't want anyone else." Could he think I might mess around with his son because I'm willing to try this with him? "It's just...you don't expect me to go running like this, do you?"

I rub my palm along the outline of my hard rod, the relief instant, but the after effect so much worse.

He crosses his arms, his eyes moving down the length of my body. "I do. I expect you to do what I tell you, when I tell you. Consider this your punishment for disappointing me earlier."

Punishment. Shit. I'd asked for it, and here it is. Only, this isn't punishment, it's torture. Bad enough I have to admit how much I want to belong to another man, but to want him and be denied?

"Now, move your ass, Mr. Montgomery, before I make it so sore you won't be able to sit for a week."

He points to his office door. I hesitate for a moment, considering if it'd be worth the beating just to have his hands on me again.

"Yes, sir." I do as he says instead, in the hopes that, if I obey and am good, he'll reward me.

Soon.

Chapter 4

The run is brutal.

Not the distance, although ten miles is not for pussies. No, it's that every single goddamn step, jostle, and leg movement brings with it a fresh wave of lust. By mile two, it borders on painful, and I wonder if I can keep up. By mile three, it dulls, and I'm both grateful and relieved.

By mile five, Griffin notices I'm easily keeping pace, obviously *not* focusing on my discomfort. That's when he reaches out and strokes me with the back of his hand, ever so fucking lightly, not breaking a single stride.

He might as well have punched me in the nuts.

I almost trip over my feet, eat shit on the asphalt track that goes around his neighborhood. I right myself, he laughs, and fuck him. I'm starting to have serious doubts about agreeing to be his when he suddenly pushes me off the track, into a grouping of trees, and fucks my mouth with his tongue until I almost cum in my shorts.

When he releases me, I fall. My hands and knees are nice enough to catch me. But they don't appreciate the debris and dirt making this position painful.

"As much as I want to see you on all fours, now isn't the time. Get up. We're only halfway done."

Only halfway? The complaint sticks in my throat the same way I wish he'd stick me in his throat.

"Yes, sir," I somehow manage to say as I push to stand and take off after him, at his pace.

Every mile after that, the back of his hand makes contact with my crotch. By the time we reach his house, I could cry, my balls hurt that much.

When we get back into his office, Mr. Hart locks all the doors, pulls the curtains and blinds, cuts us off from the outside world.

"Take off your clothes," he commands after flicking the final lock. "Place them in a pile by the door."

I swallow, my stomach trying its damndest to crawl up my throat. "All of them?" I ask, my voice squeaky.

"All of them. I want you completely nude." His eyes do a quick trip around my body like I'm a racetrack he's about to drive at full speed. "The longer it takes you to undress, the longer everything will take." He stares at my painfully engorged bulge, his point clear.

I've never undressed so fast in my entire life. I have a feeling, with Griffin Hart, I'm about to turn a lot of *never befores* into *firsts*.

It's only when I'm standing completely naked in front of him, everything about me on full display, the cool air nipping at all that exposed skin, that I remember to be self conscious.

My hands immediately cup my dick, try to block my full sac. It's pointless, because I'm too hard, but the part of my brain trying to hold onto the notion I'm straight needs to make a show of it.

"Hands behind your back." His command comes quick, with a sternness I haven't heard before.

I hesitate, the war inside raging about which side I'm on. The pause is a mistake.

Faster than I can track, Griffin has his hand around my throat, my back pushed against the wall. I grunt when the air is knocked from my lungs. My hands instinctively wrap around his wrist and forearm.

At least he got what he wanted. Me, uncovered.

A nanosecond after that thought registers, a vice tightens around my nuts, choking the blood flow. With how full they are, how turned on I am, it's too much pressure.

"Fuck!" I try and say, but the word is garbled against the hand around my throat.

"Listen, and listen carefully, Mr. Montgomery. I'm only going to say this once."

He waits for me to nod, to acknowledge that I heard him.

"Either we're doing this, or we aren't. No more of this back-and-forth shit. Are we clear?"

I nod.

He releases his grip on my throat so that he's no longer cutting off circulation and my airway, but he doesn't remove his hand, and he doesn't loosen his grip around my sac.

"You don't have to define what you are. Gay. Straight. Bi. I don't give a shit about those labels. When you're with me, they don't matter. The rest of the world doesn't exist. What matters is that you want to be here. Do you want to be here, Mr. Montgomery? Again, either answer is fine. If you want out, tell me now, and everything will go back to the way it was. Zero strings."

This is it. He's giving me an out. Free and clear. But I don't want out. Every nerve in my body tells me as much. Every skin cell where his connects with mine begs for more.

"I don't want out, Griffin." I say his first name because I need him to know I'm in. "I want you. I've wanted you since day one." Releasing my grip on his forearms, I move my hands to his chest, fist his sweaty shirt between my fingers.

He kisses me. *God*, I didn't expect him to, and it's the perfect response. I feel the pull of his lips and tongue all the way to my toes. All the way to my marrow. All the way in me.

When he pushes away, he's breathing as hard as I am. Finally, mercifully, he releases his vice grip on my nuts, rubs at the sensitive flesh and orbs beneath.

"Now we have that established, I should probably give you a safe word." He rests his forehead against mine, and everything about him envelops me. His presence, his heat, and the subtle way he smells like the perfect mixture of sweat and faded cologne.

"Safe word?" It's weird, because, with what we're doing, how far over the line I'm willing to go, those two words don't seem to fit. The idea of belonging to him far from safe.

"Yes. Safe word. When you're with me, you do what I say, when I say. It's my job to push your boundaries. It's your job to tell me when I've pushed too far."

"I'm way past too far," I admit.

"No." He shakes his head, his full bottom lip curling with the word. "You aren't even close. But you will be. In this type of relationship, dom and sub, you give me all the control, but you hold all the power. Do you understand?"

I shake my head. "No, sir."

He grabs my nuts again. I let out a noise half way between a screech and a groan. If I thought he was rough before, it was because he hadn't yet brutalized me in this particular way.

Tears prick my eyes. My dick, hard as it is, wants to crawl inside me. Hide and never come out. My balls, too, but they aren't going anywhere.

"Grif—" I choke on his name, unable to get it out. Unable to do anything but focus on the blinding pain. "Too. Far." I finally manage to say.

He lets go. The relief is instantaneous.

"That's how this works," he says, but it's hard to focus through the pain radiating up my spine, driving ice picks into my skull. "You tell me when it's too much. I stop."

If he's waiting on a response, he won't get one. I can hardly breathe, let alone get my voice to work.

"Aiden?"

Shutting my eyes so tight they ache, I clench my fists and will the radiating torture to subside enough to answer. Turns out, my will is pretty fucking weak at the moment.

Something like a sob breaks free from my chest. Dropping to his knees, Griffin takes my cock into his mouth while his fingertips try and massage out the pain in my sac.

Suddenly, everything comes alive. And because I'm so sensitive, the sensation of his lips and tongue against my length are magnified a thousand times.

"Oh, God," I choke out, only this time for a different reason.

The orgasm I've been denied all day rises fast and hot. My toes curl. My core tightens. My fingernails scratch at the wall behind me. It doesn't even occur to me to be bothered that another man is giving me head for the first time in my life.

The instant before his mouth tips me over the edge, Griffin pulls away. His lips trail a gentle path down my shaft. He sucks one testicle into his mouth, releases, then takes in the other one.

Using my thighs for leverage, he pushes to standing. "Better?" he asks. The way his lips twist, he knows the answer.

"No. It's so much worse, sir."

He plants a single, chaste kiss against my lips, and I can taste myself on him. "Have you ever been denied before?"

"Never. Sir."

He runs his fingers over his mouth to wipe away his spit. "Makes everything so much more...*intense*, don't you think?"

"That's, uh, that's one word."

"I'm going to hit the shower." He whips his sweaty shirt over his head and tosses it to the floor. "That's all for today, Mr. Montgomery."

"All?" I've never realized how much emotion someone could put into one word. In three short letters are sentiment enough to fill a fucking library. "Please, Grif—Mr. H—Sir. Please don't make me leave. Please don't leave me like this."

I don't touch my dick, don't dare, because I know the instant I do, I'll explode.

"You're right." He draws out the words, pretending as if he only just remembered he forgot something. A large, hard, painful something. "You can't leave yet. I haven't chosen your safe word."

He taps his lip, the muscles in his chest jumping with the motion. "I've got it."

Fucking me with nothing more than his eyes—in the way I wish he would with his body—he slowly reaches out, snakes his hands around my waist, and grabs two handfuls of ass.

"Straight. Your safe word is straight."

Chapter 5

When Mr. Hart lets go of my ass, turns from me and heads to his private bathroom, I think I might actually die.

The bathroom door closes. The shower turns on. I sink to my knees, my dick dripping with precum.

I bite back the scream working its way up my throat, worried even that could make me go off.

I've never been this turned on before. No. Turned on doesn't seem like the right words to describe the total and complete awareness every molecule in my body has for the thing between my legs.

By the time Griffin turns off the shower, I'm no longer a man. I'm no longer anything but a pathetic, weak, desperate sensation waiting for the right stimulus.

He takes his time in the bathroom. I don't know how long I kneel on his floor in the middle of the office. I don't care. I'd stay here overnight if it meant relief.

"You still here?"

Mr. Hart's voice sounds from somewhere behind me, close to my ear. I didn't hear him finish up in the bathroom, or open the door. My brain is too preoccupied with the pain making me feel like I'm burning alive, the chosen fire lust.

"Aiden?" His voice sounds again, tone firm. He snaps his fingers in my face, but I can't look at him. Can't move.

"Say something," he demands, "or I'm going to think that I broke you."

He did break me. He's broken everything.

I try to get my voice to work, try to force air from my lungs, up my throat, to activate my vocal chords. It's a poor attempt.

"What was that?"

Griffin kneels beside me in nothing but a pair of flannel sleep pants. No shirt. He smells like expensive soap and citrus shampoo.

"Straight," I finally manage to croak. "Straight," I say again, louder this time. "Fucking STRAIGHT!" I shout, hoping that release will help ease the one denied me.

Mr. Hart places his fingers underneath my chin, lifts my face until I'm looking into his. The feel of his skin on mine sends a shudder through me. My dick spasms. More precum leaks out, joining with the string leading to a small puddle on the floor.

"Is it too much?" he asks, his face and tone both serious.

I nod.

"Okay," he says, and sounds almost gentle, caring, when he says it. "But cuming will cost you."

"Fine," I answer, no hesitation. "I'm willing to pay anything."

"I know."

I probably should be worried about the grin that tilts his lips, makes him even more painfully handsome. But I'm too consumed with the need to release to think of something as silly as self preservation.

Letting go of my chin, Griffin brings his hand to the back of my neck. He grips me hard, pulls me into a kiss. I could go off just from that. But when he reaches his other hand between my legs, grabs hold of my dick and jerks me hard, I erupt.

My balls tighten. The muscles in my core turn to stone. Like the sudden vacuum of space, my orgasm sucks every molecule of need and denial into it, pulling from depths within me I never knew existed.

I've never cum so hard, so fast, in my entire life. The orgasm is blinding, and for a moment, I'm convinced I lose consciousness.

I scream. No. I roar.

I hope to fuck this office is soundproof, or I'll have a lot of explaining to do to Geo, or whoever else might be here.

Finally, when enough of my primal, base desire has made a mess of the floor beneath me, I start to feel almost human again. Griffin pulls his hand from my cock and uses the one wrapped around the back of my neck to push my face into the floor.

I'm not fast enough to stop what's happening, too spent for my reflexes to work properly. My cheek crashes into the ground, smearing into the mess I made.

"We always clean up after ourselves." Mr. Hart's voice is calm and stone cold. "Don't leave a mess, Mr. Montgomery."

I try to push to my feet, to get a towel from the bathroom to clean up my release. Griffin holds me in place.

"Where do you think you're going? You aren't permitted up until you've licked every drop of your cum off the floor." He raises the hand that jacked me off in front of my face. "Off my skin. Understand?"

Shit. I do understand. That's the problem.

He wants me to eat my own cum. Off his floor. Off his hand.

I try to glance at him, see if he's joking. But who the hell am I kidding? Of course he's serious. I don't need to see his face to know that.

I want to resist. Tell him, "Fuck, no." But with the fresh pain of my recent release still present, I know that's something I never want to feel again. If I refuse him, I have zero doubt Griffin will do just that. Or worse.

I shudder thinking about *or worse*, and slowly flick my tongue out into the pool of my now cold seed. It's disgusting. I gag a few times, but with Griffin's hand wrapped around the back of my neck, his grip insistent and unyielding, I know I don't really have a choice. Not if this is the game I want to play with him.

And fuck, I've never wanted to play anything this much in my life.

I don't know how long it takes me to clean my mess. All I know is that, eventually, I get every last drop. By the time I do, my dick is hard again.

Mr. Hart wraps his hand around my erection. "Want to get off again?" he asks, but I know better than to say yes or I'll be cleaning it up a second time. Eating my own cum once in a night is all I can take.

"No, sir. I'm good."

He laughs, swipes his thumb along my lower lip where some of my release still lingers. "That you are, Aiden."

I'm surprised when he pulls me in for a kiss. I know he can taste my cum in my mouth, but that doesn't seem to stop him.

The kiss is over as quick as it starts. Griffin pushes to his feet, the bulge in his sleep pants level with my face. I swallow thickly, not sure where this could go. If he'll shove his cock into my mouth and make me eat his cum next.

A thrill rockets down my spine, engorging me more. I'm spent, tired, and sore from being tense for so long. But if he wants me to get him off, I would. I'd eat his cock and drink him down if he demanded it of me.

It couldn't be worse than licking my own spent release off the floor.

"D-Do you..." I lick my lips, my eyes locked on his crotch. "Uh, do you want to get off, sir?"

"I do, and I will." He palms his dick, the fabric of his pants outlining his large size. "You think you're ready to go from straight to sucking me off?"

"I'm not sure, but I'm willing to try. Sir."

He stares at me for a long time. Too long. Just when I think he'll tell me no, deny me this opportunity to pleasure him in a way my body seems to want to, he steps closer so he's within reach.

"Okay, Aiden. Let's see what you trying looks like."

Sitting up on my knees, I tuck my fingertips into the band of his pants and pull them down over his bulge, his corded thighs, and finally to his bare feet. When his dick springs free, it hits me in the face.

There's something perversely satisfying about being whipped by him, even if by accident. I'm his sub. I belong to him. That action, along with so many others, proves it.

Bringing one hand to his sac, I cup his balls, roll them around on my palm. They're warm and so soft, unlike the man they belong to. With my other hand, I wrap around his base, angle his cock toward my mouth.

He moans, his head tilting back, when I flick my tongue out to taste him. I expect to hate the salt and tang of his pre-cum, to be grossed out at the fact I'm about to give my first ever blowjob to another man.

Neither of those things happen. The instant his flavor coats my tongue, I want more. I want him deeper. Putting more pressure on his sac, I slide my lips down and around his shaft until his head hits the back of my throat.

His toes grip the floor. His hand wraps in my hair, barely long enough to grab hold of. He curses, says my name, then grunts.

It feels better than amazing to know it's my mouth giving him this much pleasure. I set a pace that I would like, use my hand around his shaft to twist and pump. He makes a few corrections, teaching me exactly what he likes.

I pay attention to every aspect of his body. The way his muscles bunch and move in both his legs, abs, and shoulders. The sounds he makes when I run my tongue along the slit in his head. The way his cock engorges, telling me he's close before his words do.

"I'm going to cum, Aiden. You're going to swallow me."

I nod, use my tongue to create more pressure, and cup his balls more forcefully. Nothing like how he did to me, but enough to heighten the sensation of everything else.

With his hand on the back of my head, Griffin shoves deep, his tip hitting the back of my throat. I ready myself both mentally and physically to drink him down. Sucking cock is as much a head game as it is anything.

He curses, louder this time, says my name, and unloads.

The first squirt hits the back of my throat hot and fast. It's reflex to swallow, to take what he's giving and want more. After the next two squirts, I time his release with my hand so I'm stroking the part of his shaft not in my mouth.

I don't dare stop sucking, dare stop stroking, until his dick quits jerking and his release no longer hits my tongue—his flavor bursting across it in the kind of addictive taste that would make me happy on my knees every day from now on.

When Griffin catches his breath, he slides out of me, still hard but slowly coming down. "That was...impressive," he says, hand still in my hair, glossed expression in his eyes. "You sure that was your first time giving head?"

"Yes, sir."

Releasing me, he grabs his pajama pants from around his feet and pulls them up, then helps me stand.

"How was it?" he asks when I'm to my feet, still completely naked and now hard as a fucking rock.

"It was..." How *was* it? "Um, it was scary at first, because I didn't know what to expect, didn't want to disappoint you. But once I tasted you, felt you in my mouth, I wanted more. I wanted to please you."

Griffin's gorgeous lips split into the kind of grin that sets my blood boiling. "You pleased me, Aiden." He juts his chin toward the bathroom attached to his office. "Now, go take a shower, and take care of that." His gaze flicks to my hard cock.

I want to beg him to take care of me again, even if it means eating more cum. But he gave me an order, and I've pushed boundaries enough for one night.

The heated spray of his shower feels amazing on my flesh, made sensitive by everything that happened, by the impending second release of the night. I take my time, touch myself, wash myself, touch myself again. I tease, prolong, determined to be able to last longer next time.

When I do finally go off the second time, it's to thoughts of Mr. Hart. Of his cock in my mouth, of what I imagine it'll feel like in other places.

Shutting off the water, I step out and find he's left me a towel and a change of clothes. Geo's clothes. I hesitate before putting them on, not sure how I feel about wearing the clothes of my friend, and the adult child of the man I'm...what? What are we exactly?

We haven't fucked yet, so we aren't lovers. I'm his employee, yet so much more than that. I belong to him. I'm his. Maybe that's all the label I need.

When I finally exit the bathroom, Mr. Hart is at his computer. "Hope the clothes fit," he says. "I know Geo's thinner than you, but it was the best I could do short notice."

"No worries," I say, wishing he'd given me something of *his* to wear instead.

"It's okay to admit it's a bit weird," he says, still typing away on his computer, not looking at me. "After what we just did, me putting you in my son's clothes probably feels awkward."

He spares me a glance, grins, then goes back to what he was doing.

"Why, uh, why did you give me Geo's clothes instead of something of yours?" I get the nerve to ask, and fuck. Do I sound like a whiny bitch? A clingy girlfriend wanting the guy's oversized shirt to wear to bed? So I can surround myself in his scent?

He stops typing, but his eyes stay fixed on the screen. "I can give you something of mine if you wish, if you think you could explain to your family why you're wearing your boss's lounge wear."

Uh, no. I couldn't. Nor would I want to. "Good point, sir."

I gather up the pile of dirty, sweaty clothes I placed by the door and grab my phone and keys from the side table. My thumb accidentally hits the screen, lighting it up. I have fourteen text messages and six missed calls.

I worry something's wrong. That someone got hurt, or worse. Pressing on the icon for my messages, I read the first few. They're from my father, and I was right. Something is wrong. Someone's about to get hurt.

That someone is me. That something was dinner with Lily and her family.

"Shit!" I check the time on my phone. Sure enough, it's almost nine. "I-I'm sorry, Mr. Hart. Sir. I, uh, have to go." I put my hand on the doorknob, but stop. "I mean, am I excused?"

He looks up from his computer, his eyebrow cocked in a way that says he's concerned. "Everything okay?"

No. It isn't. But I don't want to have to explain to him that I missed an arranged dinner date with my future wife and her parents.

"Yeah. I just...uh, my parents asked me to come home for dinner, and I forgot. My dad gets pissed when he doesn't get his way, and my mom hates to be disrespected."

Understatement of the goddamn century.

Taking his time, Mr. Hart pushes away from his desk and stands. My nerves kick into overdrive, everything inside me screaming to get home, to try and make this right. But how?

What am I supposed to tell my father? That I'm late because I was too busy giving head to my boss? That he denied me an orgasm so thoroughly I was willing to lick my own cum off the floor? That I don't want the life they have planned? That I like men?

It's that last thought, more than anything, that ices my veins. I could never tell him that. Tell him I'd rather be with Griffin. My new boss, and college buddy's dad.

"I'm sure your parents will understand," Griffin says, his voice calm, like the rest of him. Me? I feel like a caged animal. Trapped, the way I always am when I think about my family's expectations for me. "Just tell them you were working late."

"I-I will. We were." I grip the doorknob tighter. Mr. Hart's eyes flick to my hand, then back to my face. "It's just, you don't know my father. Making him angry is never a good thing."

An unreadable expression flickers across Griffin's handsome face. "Then don't keep him waiting, Aiden."

"I won't," I say, flinging open the door harder than I intend. "Thank you, uh, sir. See you later?"

Griffin's lips pull into the slightest frown. "See you Monday, Mr. Montgomery. Have a good night."

Chapter 6

The drive back to my house takes ten minutes less than it should. Only by some miracle do I not get pulled over, or get into an accident.

Gathering the dirty clothes from my car, I sprint to my front door. I'm about to put the key into the lock when it opens.

My father's shape looms in the doorway, denying me entrance. I open my mouth to explain, to lie about getting caught up at work, when my father's hand wraps around my throat, cutting off my words and air.

He slams me against the side of the house. The clothes I was carrying fall to the porch. My hands instinctively go to his wrist. His forearm.

It's the second time tonight I've been manhandled like this, and only once have I wanted it.

"Do you think your future is a goddamn joke?" Spit flies from my father's lips, lands on my cheeks. "Do you think your mother and I haven't worked our asses off, sacrificed everything, for you? To give you a life? An education? A future family?"

I tap against his arm with my palm, my way of begging him to let me breathe. When I think I might pass out, he lets go. I fall to the ground, choke and cough, almost vomit. My throat burns. My eyes water. I want to roll into a ball, hide from him. Be a coward like I always have.

There's something about the way my father puts his hands on me that's always made me afraid of him. But when Griffin does it, I crave more. Want it. Fuck, I like it.

So, what's the difference? Why do I want it rough from Griffin, but hate it every time my father violates my trust with his spoil the rod bullshit?

Trust. That's the difference.

I trust Mr. Hart to have my best interests in mind at all times. Like he said, he has all the control. I have all the power. There's balance in what we have that's missing with my father. He has all the control and power, and he hates sharing. Hates when I tell him no, that I might have ideas and desires of my own that don't align with his.

The scuffling of feet draw my attention to the doorway. My mom's there, apron still wet from doing the dishes, look of disappointment planted firmly on her face. Sometimes I think her features are stuck in that mode, I so rarely see her smile.

"You've disgraced me, Aiden," my father says. "Embarrassed your mother. Disappointed Lily and her family."

"You could've at least called. I had to make up excuses as to why you weren't here." My mother joins in the verbal lashing. "You know how much I hate to lie."

"I know how much you both hate to look bad," I mutter, not quietly enough.

"What did you say, boy?" My father cocks back a fist.

"Not here." My mother puts her hand on his arm, gently pulls him away. I'm under zero delusions it's because she's trying to help me. No, it's that the neighbors could be watching, and if there's anything my parents care about, it's what other people think of them.

That's why it's such a cardinal sin to make them look bad by not showing up for dinner. By not following their strict letter of the law in every aspect of my life.

"I'm sorry," I say, ready to be done with this, even if it means giving in to their demands. "I'll apologize to Lily tomorrow. We can arrange another dinner, and this time I'll help you cook, Mom. Okay?"

My mom flicks her disapproving gaze to me, nods once, and heads into the house. My father isn't so easy to win over.

"Do you have anything to say for yourself?" my father asks as I pick up my clothes off the ground. "And what the hell are you wearing?"

He pinches the fabric of Geo's t-shirt between his fingers. Thankfully, the pile of clothes in my arms covers the giant white skull with the band name *Danzig* emblazoned on it.

"I told you, I was working. My boss and I went for a run. I didn't have anything to change into, so his son let me borrow some clothes."

"His son?" My father shakes his head. "You mean the faggot you went to college with?"

I wince at the word. "I don't see what him being gay has to do with anything. I was working late. He let me borrow some clothes."

My father studies my face, and I swear he knows about everything I've done with Mr. Hart. Can see it in the guilty lines of my expression. Read it in the depths of my eyes. Smell it on my skin.

"I don't like you being around that lifestyle. I mean, what kind of a man raises his son to be gay? He can't be that fucking smart if he can't keep his family in line."

"He isn't smart," I say, ready to defend Griffin from my dad's judgmental bullshit. "He's a genius, Dad. CEO of a Fortune 500 company he built from the ground up." *Unlike you*, I want to add, but know better.

My father grunts, scrubs his hand over his face. "Well, I'm going to have a talk with your boss. He needs to understand that family comes first, that he can't just keep you at all hours. You have obligations."

Fear freezes the breath in my lungs. "N-No. You can't do that."

"I can, and I goddamn will," he spits back at me and grabs my arm, shoving me inside the house.

I trip over the threshold, but right myself. He bullies his way inside after me, slams the front door. A small part of me can at least be satisfied that my mom won't be happy with him for making too much noise, drawing attention by being loud.

"I'm not a child. I'm an adult," I say, the words hard to get out, the look on my father's face enough to choke me a second time.

"If you're an adult, then fucking act like one. Act like you care about this family, about what your mother and I have sacrificed so you can have a better future."

A wave of something like bravery and backbone washes through me, a bit of newfound respect for myself. A gift from Mr. hart.

"Whose idea of a better future?" I say, voice shaking with equal parts anger and fear. "Yours? Because it sure in hell isn't mine."

I don't see the hit coming, though I should've expected it. Doesn't make it hurt less.

Pain explodes across my jaw. The force of the blow spins me around. I hit the wall behind me, then drop to one knee, determined not to go all the way down. The clothes in my arms spray across the living room floor, same as the blood from my lip.

"You ungrateful fucking brat!" My father's deep voice vibrates the air, detonates the nerves along my spine like tiny cluster bombs destroying my resolve. "I'm the man in this house. You do what I say. I'll get this lesson through to you, one way or another, Aiden."

Throwing his hands into the air, my father stomps down the hall, slams his bedroom door. My mother comes in, not to check on me, but to make sure I know I have to clean up the blood and fast, before it stains.

Using my dirty shirt to wipe my lip, I grab the cleaning products from under the sink and scrub the part of the couch and floor stained red from the proof of my parents' love.

My father's always been hard on me, but he didn't start getting violent until I was in high school. My mother, ever the faithful wife, always backs him up instead of talking about the issue.

I worry something's wrong with him, in his brain. He's always been an asshole, but not like this. Then again, I've never really stood up for myself before. I still haven't, not really, and I'm not sure I have the heart, or the balls, to see what that cluster fuck would look like.

After tossing my clothes in the laundry, and getting some ice for my swollen lip, I text Lily, deciding it's better not to wait to apologize. Maybe it'll win me points with my parents. Smooth things over as much as they can be.

Her text comes back almost immediately.

Lily: *Don't worry about it, Aiden. I know you're busy with work. Please don't make a big deal out of it, okay?*

Tell that to my parents.

Me: *Let me make it up to you.*

Lily: *You really don't have to.*

Me: *Yes, I do. My parents would flip if I didn't.*

Lily: *Don't you ever just...*

Lily: *Nevermind. How about Sunday?*

I stare at her text, wanting to know what she was going to say. I don't dare push. Even though she's going to be my future wife, I don't really know Lily that well. Every time we get together, it's pleasant enough. Surface. Safe. Most of the time, our parents are around, and they drive the conversation.

I wish Lily was someone I could talk to. Ask what's really on her mind. Tell her the truth about me. But she isn't. And no matter how much I want her to be, she isn't what I want. Despite what my father thinks, I'm not sure a future with her is even what I need.

Me: *Sunday it is.*

Chapter 7

Monday comes around way too fast, and I begin to wonder if I should start hating them like everyone else.

Dinner with Lily was, as expected, pleasant. Even though we barely spoke to one another, our parents had no problem telling us what our future will look like. Sometimes, I think it's our parents in this relationship, instead of me and her. If you can call what we have a relationship.

One of the few times we did speak, she asked what happened to my face. My father answered for me, told her I got hit by a piece of equipment at the gym at work.

Despite the copious amounts of ice I'd put on it, and triple antibiotic ointment, there's still a bruise and scab from the healing cut across my lower lip.

I won't be able to hide this from Mr. Hart. Hopefully, he has me run errands all day so I don't have to lie to him about what my father did. Face him after what we did together.

The first text from him comes in ten minutes before eight, and they don't stop. I lose myself in the rhythm of the day, grateful I'm getting my wish. After dropping off dry cleaning, delivering important papers, coordinating meetings with clients, and even getting a gift for one of the people in the office, I start to believe I might actually skate through the day without having to face him.

Sir: *Meet me at my home office. Bring lunch from my favorite deli.*

I stare at my phone, willing him to text me back. Tell me he's changed his mind. Give me the day off instead.

It's too much to hope for.

After stopping to get food, I pull up to Mr. Hart's estate, because the word home isn't large enough to encompass the massive size of the property. Geo's car is in the driveway, which surprises me. I haven't really seen him since graduation.

He's been busy working on some tech project with a couple of people he met at school. He told me about it, but I glazed over when he went into computer geek speak. It's a language I never really learned. He's fluent, has to be considering Computer Science was his major.

The clothes I'd borrowed from Geo are on my back seat. I grab them so I can return them, then let myself into the house using the key Mr. Hart gave me. I'm halfway to the kitchen when Geo's voice stops me.

"Aiden, what's up? Haven't seen you in a while. How's the job with my dad going?"

I hold up the bag with Mr. Hart's lunch and grin. "It's going."

"Dude?" He freezes, eyes locked on my face, on my busted lip and the bruise underneath. "What the hell happened to your face? Did you get into a fight?"

A fight. Yeah, it's as good an excuse as any, and it's almost true. I'd gotten my ass kicked by my dad, didn't defend myself. If that can be considered a fight, then, "Yep."

Geo rolls his eyes, stalks over to me, tries to touch my cut. I flinch and take a step back. "You are like the epitome of straight white boy. Let me guess. You got this at a bar because you hit on some dude's girlfriend."

Not even close.

I nod.

"Who are you to talk?" I eye his black leather pants, chain wallet, dyed black hair, and ripped, sleeveless The Cure t-shirt. "You're the epitome of emo, white boy goth. Punk Rock called. They want the 1980s back."

Geo sticks out his tongue, the fake gem on top of his piercing catching the light. "Guess we're a bunch of dickhead cliches, huh?"

I crack a grin, because he has no idea. When I do, Geo pulls me into a hug, squeezes my ass. He smells like pot, patchouli, and regret.

The hug and ass-grab isn't unexpected. He's always liked touching me. I always used to let him because it was harmless. But now, with things the way they are with his father, it feels awkward. Wrong.

"I've missed you, man. Missed hanging out. *Getting drunk.*" Geo steps closer, the front of his body rubbing against mine, his hands pulling my hips forward.

The implication is clear. He wants me. He's wanted me for the year we've been friends.

It never bothered me before because I'd always been curious but too closeted to ever cross that line. Plus, I'm not attracted to Geo. Not interested. I let him kiss me *once* because I was drunk. I wanted to know what it would feel like to have a man's mouth on mine.

Now I know. I've experienced so much more than that with someone I actually do want. Do find attractive. Someone I'd do anything for.

I pull away from Geo, from his misplaced desire, and head toward the kitchen to get a plate for Mr. Hart's lunch. I know he's expecting it, and I don't want to keep him waiting, or he'll keep *me* waiting.

"Okay, okay. I get it. You're straight. I'll stop pushing." The tone in Geo's voice tells me he'll never stop pushing.

Geo juts his chin at the bundle of clothes I set down on the counter next to the deli bag. "I see my clothes worked out."

"Yeah, man. Thanks."

Geo saunters into the kitchen after me, as if he didn't just hit on me, and I turned him down. That's fine. Better than fine. If he wants to pretend nothing happened, I'm happy to play along.

"So, what did my dad have you do last Friday that you needed a change of clothes?"

I shrug, trying to play off the flash of heat that burns under the surface of my skin when I remember just what his father had me doing. "About ten miles. If his last assistant was out of shape, I can see why she quit."

Geo and I share a laugh as he picks at his dad's sandwich. I swat his hand away. "He likes to keep people on their toes, push their boundaries," he says, pouting at my denial of the piece of meat dangling off the side of the sandwich. "You know?"

Geo stares at me with dark eyes; eyes that are so much like my boss's. His father. "Yeah, I do know," I mutter, mouth dry. "So, how's your project going?" I ask, steering the subject away from his dad and all the boundaries of mine he's pushed lately.

Kicking back against the counter, Geo grins in the way he always does before suggesting me and our buddies go and get into some trouble. "I'm not really supposed to talk about it. It's questionable, legally speaking. Let's just say that, you know how conspiracy people put tape over their laptop cameras because they think Big Brother is watching?"

"Yeah." I transfer Griffin's sandwich to a plate, then do the same with mine.

"It isn't Big Brother who's watching." This time, the piece of meat he steals is from my sandwich. I let him.

My frown tugs at the cut on my lip, not enough to hurt, just enough to remind me it's there. "So, you're like, spying on people?"

"I call it *surveillance*."

He winks and crosses his skinny arms over his tattered t-shirt in a pose that just begs me to judge him. It won't work. I've never judged Geo. He's always been who he is. I've always been okay with that.

"I'm trying to get my dad's company to put venture capital into it, then hopefully get a government contract."

"Cool," I say, acting like him breaking the law is no big deal. "You'll have to tell me more about it when you're allowed."

"Mr. Montgomery."

Griffin's voice freezes me in place, my hands already reaching to grab our plates.

My body's reaction to him is immediate, and I don't only mean the desire that punches me in the gut every time he enters a room.

Placing my hands behind my back, I stand with my feet hip width apart and lower my head, exactly the way he trained me. Only, this time, I angle my chin so that he can't see my lip.

"Yes, sir."

"You were supposed to be in my office ten minutes ago."

I flinch, because I know he'll make me pay for that.

"I'm sorry, sir."

Mr. Hart's gaze flicks from me to Geo. "You're on the clock, Mr. Montgomery. Fraternize with my son on your own time."

"Yes, sir."

Without another word, Mr. Hart stalks down the stairs leading to his private office.

I grab our plates, knowing that whatever he has in store for me isn't going to be fun. Geo's hand wraps around my bicep, holding me in place.

I whip my head around, to tell him to let go, that I'm working. The look on his face makes me shut my mouth.

"Is my father *training* you?" Geo practically hisses the word, the venom in his voice unmistakable.

Acid replaces my blood, burning my veins. But I remind myself to keep cool. He doesn't know anything. It's none of his fucking business.

"Of course he's training me. I'm his employee."

Geo lets go of my arm but doesn't step back. "That's not what I mean, Aiden, and you know it."

I give him my best confused look. "No. I don't know what you mean. Sorry, but I have to go. Your father isn't a man you want to keep waiting."

Geo's features relax into a blank mask. He runs his fingers through his long, black hair, his black fingernails blending in. "You're right. He isn't. Sorry I got on your case. Catch you later?"

"Yeah. Later."

I hurry down the stairs as fast as I can balancing two plates loaded with deli goodness. The door is open when I get there.

I push it open the rest of the way with my toe, and close it the same way.

Before I turn around, Mr. Hart's voice lashes at me like a whip. Maybe a whip would hurt less.

"What the fuck were you doing up there with my son?"

Suddenly, the plates feel heavy in my hands. I don't dare set them down. "Talking. Returning his clothes I borrowed."

There's that damn flush again when I think about *why* I borrowed them, followed by shame, guilt, and anger at everything that happened after.

"So, he didn't put his hands on you?" His voice sounds closer this time. Right behind me, closer. "Like this?"

Mr. Hart grabs my ass the same way Geo had, and shit. Is his whole house wired with cameras, or something?

"H-He always grabs me like that. Ever since he met me," I explain. "He thinks it's funny. I've always shrugged it off because I'm straight. Well, I, uh...he thinks I am."

His grip on my ass hardens to the point of pain. I suck in a breath, relish in the feel of the punishment. Knowing it's him giving it to me.

"No, Mr. Montgomery. You let him touch you because you lack the balls to stand up for yourself."

Grabbing the back of my neck, Griffin uses his grip to spin me to face him. I balance the sandwiches on their plates, barely. The muscles in my arms scream for relief.

I make eye contact only for a second before lowering my head. Yes, in submission, but mostly so he doesn't see my lip. As if I can hide it from him.

He grabs my chin. I cry out in pain. One of the plates crashes to the floor. He doesn't spare it a single glance, doesn't yell at me for dropping it like I expect him to. In fact, when he speaks, it's almost gentle. Soothing. Like he cares.

"Who put their hands on you, Aiden?" His breath heats the space between us. His fingers tenderly caress the bruised flesh.

My stomach twists into knots, my pulse swishing in my ears. This is it. The moment I have to lie to him. The moment I have to choose to protect my family over telling the truth to the man I care about. The man I respect. Who respects me.

"Before you answer, I want you to know you're safe." Griffin presses his hand against my chest. There's no way he doesn't feel how hard my heart pounds. "I want you to know you can tell me anything. That, no matter what you decide to tell me, truth or lie, I won't punish you for it. Do you understand, Aiden?"

I understand. He's giving me a choice. And even though he might not punish me if I lie, a part of me knows that whatever we have would be over if I did. I don't want it to be over.

"My father and I had an argument. I lost," I say, fighting for every single syllable. But as soon as the words are out, I feel...*better*. As if trapping the truth inside me made me a prisoner, and only now am I free.

Griffin blows out a breath, leans his forehead against mine. "What happened?"

It's a simple question. Two words. Nothing that should be explosive enough to destroy the dam inside. But they are.

"I was supposed to have dinner with my fiancé and her family on Friday. But, since I was here late, with you, I forgot. My parents hate to look bad, hate when I don't follow the plan they have for me. This"—I touch my lip—"was my punishment. My father's way of letting me know he's in charge."

Griffin steps back, his eyes searching mine. I miss his warmth, my entire body craving the heat of his. I don't move, though. Not unless he commands it of me.

"You're engaged." He says it as a statement, not a question, which is weird, but maybe that's his way of keeping control. Of not showing surprise.

"Yes," I admit, and it's so fucking hard to look him in the eyes. But he deserves the truth from me. "Well, sort of."

He cocks an eyebrow. "How can you be sort of engaged?"

I shuffle the plate into my free hand and try not to glance at the one on the floor I dropped. "It's kind of an arranged thing between my parents and hers. They've been telling us we're supposed to get married since high school. That, after college, we'd start our own family." I purse my lips, those words tasting sour.

"So, it isn't something you've chosen?" he asks.

"No, sir."

"It isn't something you want?"

"No, sir."

"Stop," he says. My entire body freezes. I don't even breathe. "This isn't a fucking game, Aiden. You're being abused, and you're in a relationship with someone else, two things you should've told me from the start."

"I'm not...we're not—"

"If we don't have honesty, we have nothing, Mr. Montgomery."

"I'm sorry, sir. It wasn't my intention to deceive you. I'm not hiding anything on purpose. It just didn't occur to me to say something until now."

Griffin's jaw muscle writhes like a downed livewire. "Don't call me *sir*. Right now, you aren't my sub. After this, I don't know that you will be again. I don't want to be rough with you. I don't want to push—"

"No! Please, sir. Fuck. I mean, Mr. Hart. Every part of my life is fucked up. I have no power. No balls, as you said. I haven't chosen any of it. Not my family. Not my school. Not even my future."

I push the plate with his sandwich on it into his hand, then drop to one knee in front of him, head bowed.

"But this? I choose this. I want this. Belonging to you is the only place where I feel seen. Where I feel like I have power. Where I feel like someone gives a shit about me."

"Aiden—"

"No!" I shout, cutting him off. I don't give a fuck if it's a mistake. If he makes me pay a thousand times, denies me a hundred orgasms. He needs to know how I feel.

"I want you to be rough with me. Hurt me. Punish me. I need you to. Need to know there's another reason for violence other than harm. That a man in my life who holds all the control wants to make me feel good. Wants me to be happy. I need to know that I can feel weak with someone else. That feeling like I'm nothing means something."

It's so quiet when I'm done shouting that I'm convinced he can hear my heart thundering in my chest. That he can smell the fear leaching out of my pores. The fear that I've lost him. Lost the chance to figure out what it is I really want before it's too late.

Griffin walks over to his desk, sets down the plate, then leans against it, head bowed. "Your father called me."

Chapter 8

My stomach bottoms out, same way it does on a roller coaster when you wonder if this thing will come crashing to the ground.

"He's a very *interesting* man."

"Interesting isn't the word I'd use," I admit, amazed my voice even works.

"He told me about your fiancé. Told me how important family is. How you have obligations that come first, before any job. After I got off the phone with him, I'd decided to end things with you, transfer you to a different department and let you get on with your life."

His words are like a searing, heavy slash across my chest. They cut me wide open, spilling everything out. I haven't known Griffin Hart very long. Long enough to know I want more of him. More of the freedom to explore what he can give. More of how he makes me feel strong, even when I'm on my knees.

Before I can open my mouth to beg, he holds up his hand.

"But you want to know the fucking truth, Aiden?"

My head snaps up, my eyes meeting his. "Always the truth, sir."

Pushing off his desk, Griffin stalks over to me, every step sending blood to my cock, making it hard just for him. When he reaches me, he bends down, grabs a fistful of my shirt, and hauls me to my feet.

His body crowds mine. I fight a moan at how good his heat and scent feel as they beat against me. A few steps, and my back hits the wall. Griffin's knee goes between my legs. I spread for him.

Bringing his lips to mine in the slightest touch, he says, "I don't want to let you go. I want to keep training you. Want to keep pushing you. Want to hear you beg and moan, watch you suffer when I deny you what belongs to *me*. I want to fuck your compliant, submissive mouth, and eventually, take your virgin ass. I want to mark you. Defile and ruin you for anyone else. Ever. You're *mine*, Mr. Montgomery. I'm not in the habit of letting anyone take what's mine."

Pressing me hard against the wall with his body, Griffin kisses me. He isn't gentle, and my busted lip screams in protest for me to stop. But I'm not stopping. I'll never stop, not when it comes to him.

He tangles his fingers in my hair, pulling away too quickly. "I want your dick. Take it out, now."

I do what he says, my fingers fumbling with my belt, button, and zipper. He works on his pants as well, and it's satisfying to know he's struggling, too. That he wants this as much as I do.

My cock springs free first: hard, pulsing, wanting. He reaches into the opening in the front of his pants, pulls out his thick, delicious length, rubs it against mine, wraps his fingers around both of us.

I moan when we touch. His mouth catches it as he deepens our kiss. My hands find his shoulders. I dig in. He makes my world spin with a touch, him the only solid thing.

With his hands between us, he holds our cocks together, strokes them both up and down. I'm already close, on edge from our conversation, at the thought of losing him.

"Oh, God, sir. I'm close. Please, let me cum. I'll eat it. I'll do whatever you want. Just, please don't deny me."

With his forehead against mine, the bulk of his body holding me in place, he glances down as he works us.

"I'm close, too," he finally says, and I want so bad to let loose. Let the spring wound tight around my entire life break apart. But he hasn't given me permission. More than anything, I need him to give it to me. To take control.

"I can't...sir," I say, my voice strangled by my efforts to hold out. "Please," I beg.

"Fuck, Aiden," he growls. "Cum. *Now!*"

His dick jerks against mine, his hot cum coating my stomach. My fingers dig into his shoulders. The pulsing, throbbing need wrecking me from my toes to my groin gathers into one giant ball. Like a rubber band stretches then suddenly snaps, I go off.

I'm not quiet, and I'm not restrained, as cum squirts hard from my slit, coating my shirt, his pants, hell, everywhere. But this is one mess I'm going to enjoy cleaning up.

When I stop pulsing, and the last dregs leak out of my spent dick, I drop to my knees. Bringing my lips to his pants, I lick every wet spot on his slacks, then slide up to his sac. I take him into my mouth, let my tongue trace a leisurely path up the underside of his still hard length.

He grunts when I put him in my mouth, suck hard on his head to make sure he's spent of everything he has to offer. When his dick is clean, I lick his hands, then drop down all the way to the floor to clean up his shoes.

"Damn, Aiden. I take it you like the taste of cum?"

I grin up at him as I slowly lick the top of his polished shoe. "I like the taste of you," I admit.

He pulls me to my feet. "I've created a monster, it seems." His lips brush mine, tasting our combined release. "Be careful, Mr. Montgomery, or I'll see to it you spend the next six months on your knees."

I flick my tongue out, run it along his lower lip. "If that's what you want, sir."

He grabs me around the back of my neck, his other hand fisting my shirt. "What I want is you, naked." He flicks his chin toward his bathroom. "In there."

After another fierce kiss, he lets me go. I obey his command and strip, leaving my clothes in a pile by the bathroom door. By the time I'm standing in front of the mirror, I'm at full attention, ready to go again. Ready for whatever he has planned.

Griffin leans against the doorframe, crosses his arms. "Open the top drawer, left."

I do as I'm told and slide the drawer open. Inside is an array of clear plastic pieces, one of them shaped like the head of a penis. Next to the plastic pieces is a small square box.

"Look inside the box first," Griffin says, his eyes glued to my every movement. Is he as nervous and excited about this as I am?

"Okay." I grab the box, open the lid.

Inside is a horseshoe shaped metallic band with a bar that goes straight across. It looks like a medieval torture cuff, but modern and stylized.

"What is it?" I ask, wondering if this is something that's supposed to go around...

I glance at my dick, hard and ready for him. No, it can't be for that. It's the wrong size.

Pushing off the doorframe, Griffin closes the distance to me, picks up the item from the box. "It's a screw cuff bracelet."

Unscrewing the bar, he opens the bracelet, places it around my wrist, and closes it.

"Consider this your training collar, the thing that marks you as mine. You are to wear it at all times, even when you shower. Don't remove it. It's my job to decide when to unleash you."

My dick jumps, swirls in the air. A bead of precum mixed with what was left of actual cum wets my slit, and damn. I want Griffin Hart in a bad way. The kind of way I'd be willing to walk away from my life for.

"A-And that?" I nod at the plastic pieces.

The grin that splits Griffin's kissable lips is downright wicked. "That is your chastity."

"My what?" My voice cracks. A jolt of fear tracks down my spine, making my hole clench.

"It's a cage, Aiden." He grabs out the large piece shaped like the head of my penis with a very short shaft. "It's meant to deny you orgasm. Deny you the ability to stand fully erect." He slides his hand down my length to punctuate his point.

"Why would you want to do that?" Like a poisonous snake about to strike, I try and take a step away from the thing meant to deny me pleasure.

Griffin grips my dick harder, not letting me move an inch.

"Where the fuck do you think you're going?" he asks, an amused grin on his face. "I haven't given you permission to leave. And I won't until your cage is firmly in place, locked tight." He points to the tiny lock I hadn't noticed sitting next to two plastic pegs and a semicircle ring.

Swallowing hard, I decide to beg. Maybe if I offer to do...what? Anything? Maybe he won't put that thing on my dick.

"Please, sir. I'll do whatever you want. I'll blow you. I'll eat your ass. I'll give you mine. Whatever you want. Just...fuck, don't put that on me."

Griffin's laugh vibrates off the tiled walls, slams into my chest full force. "Make no mistake, Mr. Montgomery, you'll do all of those things, and more." He twirls the larger plastic piece around his fingers. "Being caged has a way of making the sub more compliant. Eager. Willing."

"I'm already eager. Already willing, sir."

The smile drops from Mr. Hart's face. He releases his hold on my erection. "Is this a hard limit for you, Aiden? Something you're absolutely not willing to do? Because if you're *straight* on this, I'll back off."

I do want him to back off, don't want that thing restraining my dick. But the thought of outright saying no makes me feel like a huge hypocrite. I want to be with him because of the boundaries he pushes. Because I discover something about myself every time I'm with him. If I say no to this, what will I really be denying myself?

Licking my dry lips, I stare at the plastic piece in his hand. "Will it hurt?"

"It isn't painful, if that's what you mean. It's uncomfortable, designed to be a constant reminder that you're in chastity. That I own your cock. That every time you cum it's because I allow it. You'll want out, and that want will allow you to push, and explore, and discover farther than you would without it."

When he puts it that way... "Oh. Okay, well, I'm willing to try, if—I mean, if this is what you want."

Putting his hand back on my cock, Griffin steps into me, his lips skimming down the side of my neck to my shoulder, peppering kisses along the way. I shiver, because fuck if his mouth against my flesh doesn't feel amazing.

"This is what I want. And I think you'll be surprised how much you'll want it, too."

His mouth doesn't stop at my shoulder. He continues on, his tongue teasing my nipple, then lower, across my stomach.

"Hold out your hand," he says, his breath skimming across my pubes, tickling me.

I do as he says. He puts the large plastic piece meant to cage my dick into my palm. "Before I can put you into chastity, you need to be soft."

He runs his tongue along the underside of my stiff cock, the opposite of soft. I shudder and moan, and don't try to hide it. I want him to know what he does to me. Want him to see how much I need him. That I choose to be here. That I'm willing to let him lead, follow him wherever he wants to take me.

"I'm going to help you get soft, Mr. Montgomery." He flicks his tongue out, the string of precum leading from my tip to his mouth making me want to go off already. "I invite you to enjoy this, because the next time you cum, you'll have earned it."

I don't even get a, "Yes, sir," out of my mouth before he takes my breath away. His lips wrap around me, his tongue working the kind of magic I want to learn so he can feel how good this is.

With one hand gripping my sac, pulling on the sensitive orbs, stretching the thin flesh, he wraps the other around my base and twists as he strokes up to meet his mouth.

My vision blurs, white dots dance middair. My muscles harden into stone. Shit, everything about me is hard. Instead of gripping his hair, fucking into his mouth like I want so badly to, I squeeze the granite countertop behind me. My fingers cramp from the pressure, the plastic of my soon-to-be cage digging into flesh.

I cum hard and fast; too fast to warn him, too hard to even scream. When my first squirt erupts into his mouth, he eats my dick until the tip hits the back of his throat. Every time I jerk, he swallows.

It's only when I collapse against the counter, and black darkens the corners of my vision, that I remember to breathe. While I'm recovering from the most intense blowjob ever, Griffin reaches into the drawer and assembles the cage. The sound of the lock clicking echoes in my ears, bounces off the tiles.

As if I weren't his already, there's no denying it now. I belong to Griffin Hart.

Chapter 9

I scratch and adjust my crotch for the hundredth time in as many seconds as I pull into the driveway at Mr. Hart's estate.

Being in chastity sucks dirty, hairy, sweaty ball sacs. Which are exactly how mine are. No matter how many times I wash this thing, it gets funky after two days. Mercifully, Mr. Hart lets me out of it regularly so I can clean up in his private bathroom. He's always diligent about putting my cage right back where he says it belongs.

The irony of feeling like I was trapped before I met Griffin Hart isn't lost on me.

Five days. Five long, excruciating, painstakingly slow days I've been locked up. After he sucked me off in his bathroom, trapped my dick and balls in this modern day torture device, he told me the only way I was getting out of it was if I came clean with my parents and fiancé about not wanting to be engaged. He said it was the right thing to do.

I would have agreed with him whether I was in chastity or not. But, as much as I hate to admit it, he was right. Being in chastity has motivated me to move up the time table on growing a pair and facing my family, which I'm doing tonight.

I'd picked up the phone the day he locked me up, told Lily and my parents I wanted to have an engagement announcement dinner. I thought merely arranging it would've been enough to earn my freedom. But no. Griffin says pleasuring me wouldn't be right as long as I'm still engaged, or whatever the hell I am. He says that, until I break it off with Lily, he considers me a taken man. Off the market.

Never mind we've already crossed enough lines to make his point moot. Never mind him making me his sub is still him getting pleasure. And never mind that me having a break-up dinner with my family and Lily's family is a terrible idea on the best of days. But now, with how tightly wound I am? I'll be catastrophic.

Doesn't matter. What Griffin says, goes. And if he says I have to wait to empty my full, sore, very fucking blue balls, then I'll do what he says. Even with the suck of it all, being under his control feel natural. Feels right.

Letting myself into the house, I make a beeline straight for Mr. Hart's office.

"*Jesus*, Aiden. What the fuck did my front door ever do to you?"

Geo's voice is nails on chalkboard grating. It's only partially his fault. I haven't slept in two days, not restfully anyway with how ready I am to burst, and the looming truth session with my family. But there's also a tone in his voice. A judgment I've never heard from him before.

"Sorry, Geo." I motion at the door I must've slammed. "I'm in a hurry."

"It's okay, man." He gives me one of his Geo smiles, even if it's strained at the corners, like something's bothering him. I don't have time to figure out what. And, honestly, I don't give a shit.

Call me a crappy friend. Whatever. Geo's drama. Always has been. It's only now I realize I don't have to take part.

"Okay. See ya," I say before heading toward the staircase leading to Mr. Hart's private office. My own personal torture dungeon.

"Whoa. Hold up. You can't even stop a minute to say hello? Is my father really that much of a slave driver?"

Yes. He is.

I sigh, run my hands through my hair, and face Geo. "Hi," I say, deadpan expression, clearly not in the mood.

Geo clomps over to me in his half-assed laced Doc Martin boots. He stops in front of me, steps into me like he always does. "Dude, it's just a job. You shouldn't be so stressed."

"I'm not fucking stressed," I bite out before I can stop myself. My *situation* isn't anything I want to talk to Geo about.

I take a deep breath, will my nerves to calm the hell down. "Sorry, man. Guess I am stressed."

"No worries," Geo says before pulling me into one of his hugs.

Like always, the ever present perfume of marijuana and patchouli waft from his hair, his clothes. For some reason, his scent gives me a headache. Or, rather, makes the one I have worse.

Also, like always, Geo reaches around to grab my ass. I push him away, take a step back. "Stop grabbing me." I hold my hand out between us an a buffer. "I've told you I don't like it, and you touching me that way makes me uncomfortable."

Geo holds up his hands. "Relax, Aiden. I didn't mean anything by it. Shit, man. You're so uptight, you *need* a good ass-grab."

I pinch the bridge of my nose, beg my headache to go away. "I've already told you, Geo, I'm—"

Before I know what's happening, Geo's in my face, his chest against mine. Thighs, too. Grabbing the back of my neck with one hand, he pulls me into a kiss. His tongue attempts to invade my mouth. I don't let it.

Pressing my lips as tight together as I can, I try and push him off. I'm not quick enough. His free hand, the one *not* wrapped around my neck, grabs my dick.

No. Not my dick. The cage around my dick.

Pulling his mouth from mine, Geo flinches, takes a step back. His kohl-lined eyes go wide. "I fucking knew it. You're being trained. By my goddamn father."

In another life, before Griffin Hart, before I could admit what I really wanted, fear would've been the only response to such an accusation. Denial would've followed right behind.

Maybe, in some small corner of my brain, those things still happen. Maybe they always will. But right now, with my balls locked up tight, the pressure making me want to crawl out of my own skin, and me liking it way more than I ever thought possible, the first response I have to Geo is anger.

My forearm connects with his chest. I shove him back, away from me. He hits the island counter behind him, grips it for support.

"I SAID STOP FUCKING TOUCHING ME!"

The words roar from my throat, originating in some deep, hidden part longing to be set free. They're as much for Geo as they are for my father, my mother, and anyone else who's ever repressed who I really am.

We're both breathing hard when Geo's eyes lock with mine. He doesn't make a move to retaliate. God, I wish he would, and I'm glad he doesn't. He's my boss's son. Choosing sides is not a position I want to put Griffin in, but fuck if I don't want to work off some of my frustration on his face.

"You lied to me, Aiden," Geo says, his lips twisting into a snear.

"No, I didn't. I'm not gay. Well, I wasn't. I...shit, I don't know, Geo."

He tucks a lock of black hair behind his ear, the metal in his earrings winking at me, taunting me. "So, when you kissed me, when we watched porn together, you wanted more but didn't know how to ask? Or...what? Help me out here, Aiden, because I'm feeling really fucking confused and pissed off right now."

"*You* kissed *me*," I correct him. "And no, I didn't want more."

I unclench my fists, shake out the tension riding me harder than I wish Griffin would.

"Listen, I like you, Geo. As a *friend*. I'm not interested in anything more. Never have been. Not with you."

He scoffs. "Did you just fucking friend-zone me?"

"Is that a problem?" I say, pushing back more than I ever have with anyone. Maybe Geo's good practice for tonight, the real challenge being my father.

Geo crosses his arms, lets his shoulders fall forward in the type of sulk only he can pull off. "What if it is? What if I wanted to be the one to tap your virgin ass?"

"Then I'd say that's too fucking bad."

Geo stalks toward me, less swagger than he typically has. But the look on his face tells me he still thinks he's entitled to something.

When he reaches for me, I step back. He presses his lips together, narrows his eyes, and snatches my wrist. The one with the cuff Griffin gave me.

"You think you're the first guy my father's trained?" Geo eyes the bracelet as if it's something vile, twisted. "You think you're something special?"

No. I don't think I'm the first. I don't want to think about the others, and I've never asked. Never felt the need to.

Griffin Hart is twice my age. The notion that he hasn't had several lovers over the course of his lifetime is ludicrous. But I'd be a liar if I didn't admit to myself that I want to be special. That I want him to feel something for me like I feel for him.

"Oh, shit." Geo drops my wrist, his lips tilting into a mocking grin. "You caught feelings for him, didn't you?"

I don't say anything, don't take the bait. Any answer I give will be wrong.

Geo's laugh grates on my nerves, needles against flesh feel. "You are so *fucked*, Aiden. And I don't mean in any way that's enjoyable. My father's the type of man who will use you up then cast you aside, just like he has everyone else in his life. Just like he has me."

I don't know if what Geo says is true. I know I don't want it to be. But what's undeniable is that him and his father have some shit between them that's none of my business and not my fault, no matter how much Geo might want to take it out on me.

"Are we done?" I ask, my tone dialed all the way to total dick mode. "I've got to get back to work."

"Yeah." Geo flicks out his tongue, his piercing skimming along his lip. "We're done."

I turn my back on Geo, storm down the stairs to Mr. Hart's office, Geo's words still echoing in my mind. I've never really thought about the future, what kind of relationship me and Griffin would have six months from now. A year. Five.

But now that Geo brought it up, I realize I do want something more with him. Something longer term. Something that goes beyond my cuff bracelet, this fucking chastity cage, and the words *yes, sir*.

I still want those things. Right now, I can't see a time when I won't want someone to take control of me.

Not someone. Griffin Hart.

Shit. Geo's right. I am fucked.

Before my foot hits the last stair, the deep rumble of Mr. Hart's voice makes my dick pulse inside its cage. "Mr. Montgomery."

Glancing up, I notice Mr. Hart leaning against the wall at the bottom of the staircase. I don't expect him to be there, to have heard...shit. What did he hear?

By some miracle, I don't trip over my feet and fall the rest of the way down the stairs. "Sir," I somehow manage to say even though my mouth is parched. "H-How, uh, how long have you been standing here?"

Griffin pushes off the wall, straightens the cuffs of his shirt before staring at me with his dark eyes. "Long enough to hear what I needed to," he eventually says.

I lick my lips. "Uh, which was?"

His face is expressionless. I can't get a beat on him when he says, "Everything."

Damn. If he heard everything, then he heard... "I apologize for yelling at your son. For pushing him. It was unprofessional of me, and this is your house. I shouldn't have disrespected him like that."

"Stop." He holds up his hand, shakes his head. "Not here. Come."

I follow him to his office, head bowed. For the first time, I'm actually worried about my job security. Mr. Hart could fire me for what I did to Geo. If he does, where will that leave our sub-dom relationship? Is this the part where, like Geo said, he casts me aside?

The instant we're inside his office, and Griffin locks the door, I round on him, ready to beg for my job. Ready to do anything so he doesn't kick me out.

I don't get the chance.

Wrapping his hand around my neck, Mr. Hart slams me against the door. My breath is forced from my lungs, my brain frantically trying to prepare for the ass-kicking I think he's about to give. Then he kisses me.

His mouth is hot and wet, his tongue demanding, and even though I'm in a fucking cage, restrained from being fully erect, I swear I could cum.

"I'm so fucking proud of you," he says, lips still touching mine.

"You are?" My words are strangled not only because of his grip on my throat, but because he's using his free hand to unzip my slacks. "But Geo's your son."

"He is. And he can also be an asshole who oversteps people's boundaries, who pushes buttons."

No mystery where the hell he got that from.

"He needed to be put in his place, Aiden. You needed to stand up to him. Stand up for yourself." Griffin runs his tongue along the hollow of my neck, up over my Adam's apple. "Do you know how fucking hot it is to listen to you defend yourself? To hear you own who you are? What we are?"

What are we? I want to ask, but that question is quickly derailed by another, more pressing reality.

Reaching into my pants, my boss pulls out all of my bound-together parts. I moan, the sensation of his fingers against my overly full sac like a tiny island of heaven surrounded on all sides by hell fire.

"You did well," Griffin says, his lips pressed against my neck, his hand fumbling in his pocket for something. "I believe in rewarding a job well done."

Something tiny and golden reflects in the light streaming through the overhead skylight.

A key.

Griffin slides it into the lock on my cage and turns, freeing me. My dick wastes zero time testing the structural integrity of the plastic pieces that no longer have a lock holding them tightly together. With a few deft movements, Griffin removes the cage completely, and I don't think I've ever been harder.

Running his thumb along my slit, he gathers the precum that's about to drip onto the floor. He brings his thumb to his lips, tasting me, then kisses me so I can taste myself on him.

"Go to my desk, drop your pants, and bend over. Now."

His voice is stern. Hard. In control, just like he is.

My hands shake as I do what he tells me, wondering if this is when he'll pop my cherry. Take my ass and make it his.

I want it. I do. But I'm also terrified. What if I can't handle him? What if it hurts and we have to stop? What if I won't be able to please him, or I hate it and realize this has all been a huge mistake? That I'm actually straight, and how badly I want him is just a fluke?

"Relax," he says, his hands skimming down my back until he reaches my ass. His touch is gentle, opposite of what I've come to expect and crave. Although, if he were gentle like this more often, I could crave it as well.

His lips graze my ear, making me jump. "I'm not going to fuck you, Aiden. Not yet," he says, and I swear he can read my damn mind. "So, relax," he repeats.

This time, I obey. Exhaling a heavy breath, I let the tension in my muscles release in the same way I pray he'll give the rest of me release.

With his hand on my shoulder, he guides my torso lower until I'm resting on his desk. Using his foot, he spreads my legs wider. My balls drop heavy between my thighs, the pain of having them hang free more excruciating than having them bound tight.

Running his fingers along the crack of my ass, Griffin says, "You've earned your freedom. And because you finally grew a pair"—he rubs his palm, featherlight, across my tender orbs—"you've earned some relief."

"Thank you, sir."

Dropping to one knee behind me, my boss spreads my ass cheeks wide, opening me to him. I clench in anticipation of what he's going to do, and cry out when he licks my tight little hole with his talented tongue before plunging inside.

"Oh my *fuck*!" I shout into the desk, my fingernails gouging into the lacquered wood.

My dick thrums with pent-up energy. The nerve endings leading from between my legs to somewhere deep inside my core fire on all cylinders. The pleasure of his mouth eating my ass is so intense, I almost beg him to stop. The sensation is too much. Too good. Too exactly what I've been craving my entire life.

How the fuck could I ever think me wanting this was a fluke?

My legs shake with the strain of holding back an orgasm, the muscles burning in protest with the effort. "Please, sir. Oh, God. Please. Can I cum? I need to cum."

Instead of giving me permission with his words, Griffin gives it to me with his mouth. He hums against my hole, his tongue acting like a tuning fork inside my most private place. At the same time, his fingers wrap around my cock, the pressure from his grip sending me over the edge.

I cum. Hard. Harder than I ever have. Harder than I imagine I ever will.

My balls, heavy with five days worth of denial, tighten. But because they're so full, the sensation of them trying to pump out the overflow is more intense than I expect. That, and the finger Griffin shoves inside me at the moment of release, are what prolong my orgasm into territory typically reserved for women.

Or, maybe multiples are available to men, too. But I've never before had access to someone who knew how to work my body to maximum pleasure.

My body slumps against the desk, fully spent. My knees buckle, but because the desk is there, I have enough leverage to stay upright. I know I've made a mess, that I need to clean it up, but damn if I can move.

Standing, Griffin heads into the bathroom. I hear the faucet turn on and stay on for a few seconds before turning off. I wait for him to come back into the office so he can watch me eat my own release.

When he rounds the corner, towel in hand, I somehow manage to make it to my knees. I coated the side of his desk with my own brand of lacquer, my craftsmanship far more brute force than finesse.

I stick my tongue out, ready to clean up when Griffin stops me. "Here." He hands me the towel. "Use this instead."

I stare at him in confusion.

He shakes his head, a small chuckle escaping his lips. "I told you, you earned this release. Unless, of course, you *want* to lick it up." The way he says it, I swear he's challenging me.

I glance up at him through my eyelashes. I've never been much of a flirt, but being with him makes me want to try. "I want what you want, sir." I run my tongue alongside a streak of my cum.

The embers in his eyes that had been cooling since my release catch fire again. His jaw sets in a stern expression, his lips pressing thin. "Use the towel, Mr. Montgomery, or I might change my mind about fucking you."

My asshole clenches at the heat in his words. I wouldn't stop him if he changed his mind, but that doesn't mean I need to goad him, either.

After cleaning off his desk with the towel, I wash up as best I can and get dressed. My nerves around tonight are back, but at least I'm not also so sexually frustrated I could scream.

I wrap up a few work related tasks that I originally came here for, then check the time. "I should leave soon, sir. Is there anything else you need me to do before I go?"

Griffin doesn't glance up from his computer when he says, "Need, or want?"

I bite my lower lip to keep from smirking, my mind immediately going *there*. "Whatever your desire, sir."

That gets his attention.

Mr. Hart pushes away from his desk, stands, and closes the distance between us. One hand grabs my ass, the other strokes my jaw as he kisses me until my lips are sore and my dick is hard.

When he pulls away, I don't want him to, but know he has to or I'll be late to my own de-engagement dinner. His thumb traces a path down my neck, across my shoulder, along the inside of my arm, ending at the cuff. The constant reminder that I belong to him.

It might as well be a choker and a leash. Means the same thing. Maybe most people would chafe at the idea of being dominated this way, of being owned by someone else.

I'm not most people, and there isn't anything I wouldn't give to make Griffin Hart happy.

Rubbing the flesh underneath the bracelet, he rests his forehead against mine when he says, "What I desire is you, Aiden. My son said some things to you I wish I could deny. I won't, because in the past, they've been true. I've used people, haven't always treated my lovers fairly. Or my family."

He rubs his lips lightly against mine, the sensation making me shudder.

"But what Geo doesn't understand is that I'm not that man anymore. I haven't trained anyone in years, and never someone as young and inexperienced as you. I don't expect you to believe me, and it doesn't mean anything more than this: you *are* special. There's something about you, from the moment we met, that I just had to claim. Something I've longed to taste. And now that I have, I crave more."

I crave more, too. So much more, and I'm not sure what that means. For us. For me. For what happens after tonight when I have to face the consequences of who I've allowed my family to tell me to be.

"I wish you could come with me," I mutter in the miniscule space between our mouths. He could be a buffer between me and my parents. Act as the one solid thing in a life I'm about to turn upside down.

"You'll be fine." He squeezes my wrist before stepping away. My body instantly misses his heat, the scent of him wrapped around me. "If your conversation with my son is any indication, I'd say you'll have no trouble getting your point across."

"Yeah, well, Geo isn't my dad," I say before turning toward the door.

"No, he isn't. Which reminds me, I don't want you coming to the house any more."

"What?" The word rushes out, devoid of any respect or decorum. "I mean, uh, excuse me, sir."

My boss strokes his chin with his fingers. "I don't want to give Geo the chance to harass you further, or to intrude on our personal business. From now on, we'll meet at my corporate office. Understand?"

I know this is his way of looking out for me. It still feels like a punishment. Plus, this the the place where we play as much as work. Will the dynamic between us change along with the scenery?

He runs the pad of his thumb along my lower lip. "Don't worry. You'll like the other office. Promise." He winks before dismissing me with a flick of his hand. "Now go, before you're late and I have to lock you up again to teach you a lesson about being on time."

I yank open the door, resist the urge to bolt out of there. "I'm good, sir. I think I've learned enough."

Before I close the door, I swear I hear him say, "Not near enough."

Chapter 10

I step up to the door at Lily's parent's house, palms sweaty, heart racing. My parents are already here, their car parked out front alerting me to that fact.

After straightening out my clothes, smoothing down my hair, I knock. It's an excruciating eternity before Lily answers the door.

"Hey, Aiden." Her smile is polite. Her voice calm.

At first glance, she appears perfectly...fine. Like she always does. It's her eyes that give her away, that tell me there's more to her than what's on the surface.

"Everything okay?" I mutter into her ear when she hugs me.

Her hands grip me tighter, her breath catching. She glances behind her, her gaze crossing the living room to the kitchen. Seems I'm not the only person with something that needs to be said that I'd rather my parents not hear.

"Do you...uh, do you think we could talk?" She asks so quietly I almost don't hear her.

I'm about to tell her yes, drag her out of the house, drive away from here if we have to, just to get a moment with her that doesn't involve our parents.

"Aiden," her father says, stepping up behind his daughter, pulling her from my arms.

"Mr. McCabe." I reach out, shake his hand, all standard protocol. What isn't standard is the way I look him in the eyes, the way I hold my shoulders straight instead of hunching over, cowering from him like I always do.

85

No. *Used* to do.

He notices. "You seem different. This new job has been good for you?"

I crack a smile because I can't help it. "Better than good."

"Come on in." He opens the door wider, steps aside.

Lily gives me a look as I pass her and head toward the dining room. But, because I don't know her that well, I can't read her facial expressions.

Dinner smells amazing. Despite her many faults, my mother is a genius in the kitchen. Even when working in someone else's kitchen. She takes basic ingredients and makes them into masterpieces. It's a skill I envy, and one area I don't happen to take after her, though I wish I did.

When we tuck in, I can barely bring myself to eat a few bites. I'm positive the flavors should burst across my tongue. Any other time, they would.

All I can focus on is the moment when I have to stand up to my family, to Lily's, and tell them I'm not going to marry her. That what they want, I don't. That I'm my own person, I should have a choice.

Lily squeezes my leg under the table, the one I'm bouncing up and down. A nervous habit.

"Not hungry?" she mutter so our parents can't hear.

Her plate is about as picked over as mine, though I can't figure out why. Is she nervous about something? Does she want this engagement, and me breaking it off will break her somehow?

She's never really seemed all that excited about marrying me. Never seemed excited about anything. Could just be her personality, or it could be that she feels just as trapped as I do.

I glance at the head of the table where her father sits. Then the other head, where my father sits. There's no reason to put this off, and I'll worry a hole in my stomach if I wait until everyone's done eating.

Shit. Here goes nothing.

Glancing at Lily, I say, "No. I'm not hungry." Then louder, so everyone can hear, I say, "I'd like to make an announcement."

Pushing back from the table, I stand and take a deep breath, ready to say what needs to be said.

"Sit down." My father's voice is commanding in a way that leaves zero room for negotiation. "We're still eating." He motions for me to sit with his finger.

I fight every impulse in my body to obey that command. But there's only one man who owns me. Only one man whom I obey. My father isn't him.

"No. I don't think I will sit. What I have to say can't wait."

My father's fork hits the plate with a loud clack. My mother's disapproving glare slices right through me, the way it always does. Mr. and Mrs. McCabe look to my parents, then to me.

"Alright. If you wanna do this now, that's fine." My father throws his napkin onto his plate, leans back in his chair, and fetches something from his pocket.

It's a box. Small. Silver.

"Your mother and I were going to wait until *after dinner* to give this to you. But since you're stubbornly insisting we do this now..." He pushes to standing and holds out the box for me to take.

I exchange a look with the McCabe's, with Lily. They look as confused as I feel.

"Open it," he says, full of himself like he always is. Whatever's in this box is something that's going to make him and my mother look good. Seem like caring, world's best parents.

Licking my dry lips, I open the box, almost drop it the moment I do.

"This belonged to your great-grandmother Montgomery. We're hoping you'll use it when you make Lily your wife."

A giant diamond, square cut, gleaming with a yellow sheen, winks at me against a red velvet backdrop. It's gaudy, obscenely large, and obviously antique.

It represents everything I hate about my family, about this arrangement I had no say over.

I open my mouth, close it, not sure what to say, how to tell him I'm not making Lily my wife.

"That's...uh, wow." Lily's voice breaks me out of my moment. Convinces me it's now or never.

Placing the lid on the box, I hand it back to my father. "That's very generous. Thank you, but I don't need it."

My father's brow scrunches, his lips purse. "Don't need it? What, did you buy your own diamond with your new fancy job?" He sneers at the word *job*, which is hypocritical as hell.

"No. I didn't buy a diamond because I'm not going to marry Lily."

Everyone in the room freezes, like hitting pause on a movie.

"I'm sorry, Mr. and Mrs. McCabe. You've been great, and this decision has nothing to do with you. The truth is, I'm not ready to get married, and I don't love your daughter."

I turn to face Lily. "Please forgive me. I'm not trying to be cruel. You're amazing, kind, pretty, and smart. You deserve a man who will love you for those qualities, and I'm not him."

I never will be him.

Lily stares at me for what feels like forever. I want to ask her what she's thinking, apologize to her for dropping this bomb without warning.

Finally, at some unspoken cue, she buries her face in her hands and begins to cry. Her shoulders shake. She curls in on herself. Muffled mewling sounds come from between her hands.

The room finally erupts. Lily's mother rushes to her side, tries to pry her hands away from her face. Mr. McCabe and my father yell at me, then at each other. My mother defends my father, criticizes me.

I just stand there, watching the chaos our families have made out of our lives, would continue to make if we let them. I'm done letting them.

"Enough!" I slam my fist on the table. The cuff Griffin gave me smashes against my wrist, leaves a mark on the table.

The McCabes and my parents look at me as if they're only just now seeing me for the first time.

"This decision isn't yours to make. It's mine. It's Lily's." Dropping into my chair, I put my hand on her shoulder.

She hasn't stopped crying, stopped shaking.

"That's where you're wrong, son." My father's voice echoes in the small room, intimidating the molecules in the air to vibrate at his frequency. "You're going to marry Lily McCabe because I said so. Because I know better than you. Because you owe it to your mother and I to live the kind of life that will make us proud of the time and effort we've put into you."

"Why can't you be proud of me for who I am?" I ask, hand still on Lily's shoulder. "For who I want to become."

"You'll become what your mother and I fucking tell you to become, or so help me, Aiden, you are dead to me."

Mrs. McCabe recoils from my father in fear, her husband stepping in front of her to shield her. She wears a look I know well. A look I've worn my entire life.

My mother places her hand on my father's arm, her signature move to get him in line so that he'll stop embarrassing her. But it's too late for that. Their little charade is up, and I fucking hate that game, anyway.

My father stares at her hand, then at the McCabes, as if he's only now remembering where he is. That there are witnesses.

Lily's cries grow louder, bringing the focus in the room to her. I'm seriously worried something's wrong with her when she removes her hands from her face.

She wasn't crying. She was laughing. And she doesn't stop.

Her gaze pings from her parents to mine, every shift to a new shocked face bringing a fresh round. Tears streak her cheeks, her mascara smudging her eyes with dark circles.

"Lily?" I say when she clutches her stomach, tries to catch her breath.

Without warning, Lily launches herself into my arms, hers wrapping tight around my neck. "Thank you, Aiden," she says, over and over, into my ear. "I don't love you, either. I don't want to be your wife."

The knots inside my stomach that kept me from eating, loosen. The tension in my shoulders relaxes. She feels the same way I do. Of course she does. She's been just as trapped as I have.

I can't help but wonder if she has a Griffin of her own that will help set her free. I hope she does.

"We're leaving," my father announces.

"Go ahead," I say, still holding on to Lily. If they want to leave, I'm not stopping them.

A split second later, my father's hand wraps around the back of my neck, pulling me away from Lily and out of my seat. "You're coming, too. We have unfinished business, you and I, and I won't tolerate an ungrateful, disobedient child."

Child? I haven't been a child in years. But to him, that's what I'll always be.

With all pretense of being a decent human being gone, my father shoves me toward the front door, grabs me by my hair to help me to my feet when I fall.

"It's obvious to me I've gone too easy on you, son. That ends, now," he says.

Scalp burning, eyes pricking with unshed tears, I grit my teeth, determined not to cry out. I know my boundaries so much better now, and I know my father wants the satisfaction of thinking he controls me. For some reason, me holding back is me retaining that control.

Like a well-oiled abuse mechanism, my mother opens the front door and my father throws me out. I attempt to tuck and roll down the few steps leading off the McCabe's porch, but I'm not as nimble as I think I am. I hit the ground at a wrong angle. Or, rather, my wrist does.

Bones rub together in an unnatural way. Still, I don't cry out.

My mother glances around to see if anyone is watching, tries to close the door to hide from the McCabe's what is sure to be the worst ass-kicking of my life, which says a lot. Mr. McCabe reaches out, grabs the door before it can close.

"Aiden!" Lily calls to me from behind her father's protective stance.

I'd wondered if her parents treat her the way mine treat me. But the disgusted, surprised look on their faces at my father's violent outburst tells me they don't. At least, not physically.

"Mr. Montgomery, I don't think it's approp—"

"Stay out of this," my father says to Mr. McCabe in the same threatening voice he uses with me.

"This is a family matter," my mother chimes in as if on cue. "Mind your own business, tend to your own issues." Her judgmental glare finds Lily, no doubt accusing her for what just happened at dinner. "We'll tend to ours."

Before I can push to my feet, tell them not to worry, that everything's going to be okay, my father lands a kick to my stomach. I piss myself, cough up all the air in my lungs. Pain lances through me, stealing my ability to think, to protect myself.

He kicks me again before my lungs have a chance to come back online, suffocating me. That his second kick doesn't hurt isn't a good sign. Neither is the black at the edge of my vision.

"How dare you embarrass your mother and I like this."

My father's voice is little more than a growl against my ear as he yanks on my hair. My neck bends at a painful angle, my spine curving back, choking me more. In a few seconds, I'll black out. Be at the complete mercy of my parents.

"We've sacrificed everything for you," he says, his hot breath heavy against my skin. "It's a debt we intend to collect, if not from your life, then from your flesh."

Instead of letting me go, allowing my head to flop against the pavement, my father slams my face into the sidewalk. Every nerve ending from jaw to forehead shocks me with white hot pain. I think I pass out for a moment, I'm not sure.

"I'm calling the police," I hear someone say. Lily, or Mrs. McCabe. Can't tell. Everything sounds muffled as if people are shouting behind closed doors.

"Let's go." My mother's tone is unmistakable. It's the one she uses to leash my father when things get out of control where people might see. Might judge my parents as less than their idealized version of themselves.

"I'm not fucking done with him."

Somewhere in the vicinity of my lower back, my father lands another kick. But I'm drifting now, my conscious mind ready to dissociate from my body. Leave the physical to deal with physical things.

I wonder if I'd have still stood up to my parents, told them I'm not marrying Lily, knowing this would be the outcome.

A flash of Griffin's face makes me feel warm inside—or maybe that's just internal bleeding.

Yes. The answer's yes. Not for Griffin. For myself. Because, for once, my parents needed to hear the word *no*.

And to think, I haven't even told them I'm gay.

Chapter 11

In the small moment of grace between full consciousness and the mind-body connection, I find an instant of peace. An instant where my life feels, for the first time, like it's on the trajectory it's supposed to be on. Like I'm finally becoming the man, not who my parents want me to be, but who I truly am.

Then reality drops me off a ten story building. Face first.

My nerve endings are the first thing to come back online. The assholes. Why they'd want to be in a hurry to wake up is beyond me.

"Aiden?" A gruff, tired voice sounds to my right.

I try and open my eyes, get a look at the man the voice belongs to. The man I belong to. But damn if my eyelids want to cooperate. Okay, fine. Plan B.

Forcing my tongue to wet parched lips, I clear my throat. "Yes, sir."

Wow. I sound fucking wrecked. By the sound of every molecule in my body screaming in agony at once, I'd say I am wrecked.

Griffin's cologne wraps me in his familiar scent when he stands, the breeze of his movements making even the air obey him. A nearby door opens followed by muffled voices.

Someone else enters the room. A nurse by the way they talk to me, take my vitals.

"He's in pain," Griffin says to the nurse as if he's the one in pain. "Can't you give him something before you check on all that shit?"

The nurse might not appreciate being strong-armed, but he gives me the good stuff anyway.

I breathe a sigh of relief when the morphine kicks in. Moments later, the door clicks closed. Griffin takes my hand in his and sits with me, not saying a word.

"What are you doing here?" I ask in the silence between us.

"Do you want me to go?" His voice sounds defeated, exhausted in the way that tells me he hasn't slept, possibly in days.

No, that can't be right. Dinner was just last night, wasn't it?

"No!" I say a little too forcefully. My ribs let me know. "No, sir. I just...um, how did you know I was here?"

Where the hell is *here*, anyway?

I force my eyes open, make them focus on something other than Griffin Hart. The sterile walls, beeping machines, and hospital bed tell me everything I need to know.

"What do you mean how did I know?" he asks.

Slowly, as if I'm something breakable, my boss reaches out, brushes the back of his hand across my cheek.

"Aiden, you've been in a medically induced coma for three days."

Three days? What the hell?

"Bruised ribs, cranial swelling, internal bleeding, not to mention the damage to your face and jaw. You're lucky your father didn't break it."

"Lucky?" I don't feel lucky.

Running his fingers through his disheveled hair, Griffin drops his head. "I'm sorry. I didn't know things were this bad for you at home. I would've never—"

I try and sit up straighter, push to a more comfortable position. The ribs he'd mentioned were bruised do a fantastic job of telling me that themselves. I grunt, a pitiful sound.

Griffin immediately responds. He adjusts my pillows, puts his hands underneath my arms to help me sit up. He's attentive, his touch gentle, and fuck. I just might love him more for it.

The CEO of a Fortune 500 company, at my sick bed, fussing over me like I'm something special to him.

"Things weren't this bad," I say. "But that's because I'd never stood up to my father before."

I reach for the water pitcher. He pours some in a styrofoam cup for me, brings it to my lips. I smile, take a sip.

"It takes a lot of bravery to come out to your parents." Griffin's lips pinch into a thin line. "I should know. I just wish it didn't have to go this way for you."

I laugh, which is a huge mistake.

My laughter quickly turns into coughing, and from coughing into heaving breaths where everything hurts and I can't get away from the pain no matter what I do.

Eventually, I settle, and the morphine helps keep things from getting too out of control.

I can't look at Griffin when I say, "I didn't come out to my parents. They don't know I'm gay."

I can't see them, but I know Griffin's expressive eyes are burning holes into the side of my face. I don't think I've ever said those words out loud.

I'm. Gay.

I'm not sure what I thought would happen. The Heavens part. Stars align. Fireworks explode overhead.

Somehow, I thought the moment would be more monumental than it is, though maybe simply acknowledging my sexual preference shouldn't be so earth-shattering. Not for me. Not for anyone. Maybe, it just simply isn't that big of a fucking deal.

The big fucking deal tends to be other people's reactions. Other people's judgments.

"You didn't come out?" he says as if it's the most impossible thing he's heard. "I don't understand. What the hell was all this for?" He waves a hand at my entire body.

"For telling him and my mother I won't marry Lily. You want to know the funny part?"

"Yeah, Aiden, I do, because I don't see any fucking humor in this." His tone is harsh, unforgiving. I don't know if he's pissed at me, or at my father. Or both.

"She didn't want to marry me, either. She was so happy when I said I didn't love her that she hugged me, cried in my arms. You should've seen the look on everyone's face. Fucking priceless."

I crack a grin, because too much of my life lately has been serious. I'm in a hospital, homeless, not sure if I still have a job, recently broke up with my fiancé, and just admitted out loud I'm gay. Clearly, all the seriousness in my life isn't serving me.

Griffin just stares, like I've lost my mind. Maybe I have. Maybe it's the morphine. Doesn't matter. This is the first thing I've done since coating the side of my boss's desk in my own release that's felt good.

"Aiden, you okay?" Griffin asks, concerned.

"Yeah. Better than okay. Well, wait. I don't know. Do I still have a job, boss?" I smile like a stupid idiot at one of the most powerful businessmen in all of San Diego.

Griffin tries his damndest not to crack a grin, but the corners of his full lips betray him. "Yes, Mr. Montgomery. You do. Right now, it's getting better."

"Yes, sir," I say and rub my wrist where his bracelet should be.

Shit. It's gone. I panic, frantically look around in the bed, the table beside me. It isn't there, and I worry that they cut it off when they brought me in.

"Here." Griffin reaches into his pocket, pulls out the cuff. "They removed it. I've kept it safe."

When he places the cuff on my wrist, everything feels right in the world. The bracelet has become less of a collar, more of a safety blanket. It reminds me that I belong somewhere, to someone. That I have value, bring value in return.

Griffin stays with me for a little while after. But with how much noise his cell phone makes, I know he won't be able to stay for very long. I'm grateful he was here at all. He's a busy man. That he took the time means everything to me.

The next day, Lily comes to visit. Her parents are pissed at her for lying to them. Like normal, decent people, they don't beat her or throw her out.

She tells me that, after she called 911 and the ambulance took me away, officers arrested my father. He's out now on bail, awaiting trial. When he got home, my parents threw all of my belongings into the front yard.

Worried that my parents were going to have everything sent to the dump, Lily and her family had gone over, retrieved my stuff, put it in a local storage unit not far from where they live. My car is still at their house, and she was able to swipe my keys before the ambulance took me away.

When she hands me both sets of keys—one to my car, one to the storage unit—I cry. I'm not ashamed to admit that. What they did, the care they've shown me, is how my own parents should've treated me.

I spend the rest of the week healing the damage done by my father, and looking for places to live. Rent in San Diego is stupid expensive. Better than LA and San Francisco. Still, I'll have to look for a roommate situation, or a studio that's on the small side.

For now, I settle for getting a deal on a hotel room within walking distance of Griffin's office, for when they release me from the hospital. The less I have to drive, spend money on gas, the better. My job as an executive assistant pays well, but I've never been on my own before. Had to completely pay my way. I'm not sure what my expenses will be.

Finally, after I feel like I might go stir crazy, I'm discharged from the hospital. My ribs are mostly healed, and the abrasion on my face is scabbed over. The bruising on my jaw still looks gnarly, but it doesn't hurt so much anymore.

Griffin offers to send a car to pick me up, bring me to his house. I decline. I'm in no shape to face Geo, and Lily said she'd give me a ride, show me where my storage unit is located.

After grabbing some of my things, I settle into the hotel room and call Griffin like he asked me to do.

"You're not living in a fucking hotel, Aiden."

I pull the phone away from my ear, Griffin's voice piercing through the speaker.

"Hello to you, too, sir." It's impossible to keep the snark from my tone. I shouldn't goad him, not when he's so uptight. But ever since I got my ass kicked by my father, things have changed.

I've changed.

And, I'd be lying if I didn't admit I'm hoping he makes me pay for it.

"I have a condo in a high rise downtown. I keep it for clients, and for when I work late. It's lightly furnished, so it has room for your things. You're staying there."

"Is that a command, sir? Or are you asking me?"

Griffin sighs, deep and long. I can picture him running his hands through his hair, something he's done a lot more lately, ever since the incident.

"Yes. No." Pause. "I don't fucking know."

For a man who's always in charge, always has his shit together, witnessing him fall apart, even if it's just a little, is unsettling. Can he really be that affected by what happened?

I open my mouth to ask him when he says, "Your father's hearing was today."

My heart freezes, the blood in my veins running cold.

"Because it was a family matter, his first offence, and because he knew someone at the courthouse, he got off with probation and community service."

The way he says it is like some revelation. It isn't. With as many people as my parents know, I'm surprised his punishment was as harsh as it was.

"Not one fucking day in jail. Not one." The phone jostles, and I wonder how hard he's gripping it. "A slap on the wrist for putting his own son in the hospital."

Griffin huffs into the phone. I swear I can hear him pacing.

"It isn't fucking right, Aiden. What he did to you, the mess I made you walk into, it isn't right."

A piece of the puzzle that is Griffin Hart suddenly clicks into place, the picture a tiny bit clearer.

"I've spoken to my personal attorney. Unfortunately, there isn't much we can do. *Legally*. But I know a few people who—"

"This isn't your fault," I say. The words hang in the air, louder in the silence between us.

Nothing. Not even the sound of him breathing.

"This isn't your fault," I say again, to drive home that truth.

I've wondered why Griffin has been different, more on edge, powder-keg touchy. He blames himself, thinks he caused what happened. He didn't.

"My entire life has been planned out for me," I say, hoping like hell he's listening. "I've been told where to go to school, what to wear and eat, who to hang out with, who to marry, and even who I was going to be. My. Entire. Fucking. Life."

I touch my ribs where my father kicked me, lick the mostly-healed cut on my lip from where he smashed my face into the pavement.

"Even if there was no you, no denial about my sexuality, no cuff bracelet, or commands, or any other shit, it was past time I stood up to my father. I needed to do this. Had to claim what little life was actually mine, and run with it. Yes, you were the catalyst. You pushed me, made me see I could want more. Deserve more. This isn't your fault, Griffin. This isn't your fault, and it's every bit your fault, and I fucking love you for it. For pushing me, for making me grow, for making me admit who and what I want. Who and what I am."

Now I'm the one breathing hard. I just told my boss, my dom, that I love him. It's either the stupidest thing I've done all day, or the best.

"Say something," I beg when too many uncomfortable moments pass in silence. "Please, sir."

"I'm coming to see you. Give me your room number, and give me some time to wrap up some business here. I'll bring dinner. We'll talk."

We'll. Talk.

Those words choke me, make me want to take back everything I just said. I can't lose him. Not because I'm fucked if I don't have a job, which I am, but because I don't think my heart can take the beating.

"Wait, sir—"

"Tonight, Mr. Montgomery."

The line goes dead.

Chapter 12

I pace around my hotel room, do jumping jacks until my ribs hurt and I can't breathe, and bite the nail on my thumb until it bleeds.

Waiting for whatever's about to happen between me and my boss is torture. And not the good kind from him I'm used to.

A knock sounds at the door. My heart bangs against my chest just as hard.

I touch the cuff on my wrist, run a hand through my hair, adjust the t-shirt and shorts I'm wearing to look as put together as I can.

What's that saying? Fake it 'til you make it? Me being put together will take an Oscar-worthy performance.

I open the door, step to the side, head down, stance perfect, just how Griffin taught me. I won't break pose until he gives me permission.

"Aiden," he says, voice low. Soft. Not at all like the man in control I'm used to. "Look at me."

I do as he says, movements precise. I'm determined to show him how obedient I can be. That I want this, and my feelings for him don't have to get in the way. Don't have to destroy what we have.

My eyes focus on my boss standing outside my hotel room door. And holy fuck me. In a light sweater and casual but crisp slacks, he still looks like a million bucks. Several hundred million, actually.

His sharp eyes soften as they take me in, linger on the still healing bruises and abrasions. "May I come in?" he asks. *Asks.*

Shit. This isn't going to be good.

"You can do anything you want, sir," I answer, desperately trying to hold on to the sand of our sub-dom relationship slipping through my fingers.

He pushes past me, closes the door, sets down his leather bag and the paper sack of food on the dresser. The scent of greasy fries and hamburgers fills the small room—two queen beds, a small table, chair, and couch the only other occupants.

With his back to me, gaze set out the window with a view of the ocean, Griffin says, "Did you mean what you said on the phone?"

"Do you mean when I said what happened wasn't your fault?" I hedge, not ready to admit to the other thing just yet. "Yes. I meant that. What happened with my parents wasn't your fault."

"That's not what I was referring to, and you know it. Do you love me, Mr. Montgomery?"

Classic Griffin Hart. Right to the damn point. The least I can do is give him the same courtesy.

"Not if it'll cost me everything I have with you, sir."

Griffin huffs out a breath, his shoulders slumping forward. When he finally turns to face me, I think he might yell at me. He looks pissed, and I don't know what I've done, what I can do to calm him down.

With the movements of a man with purpose, he crosses the room, closes the distance between us. I step back until I hit the wall. He keeps coming.

Blood swishes in my ears like river rapids when he presses the entire length of his body against mine. He's taller than I am, and the fact I'm cowering makes him even taller.

My desire for him burns so hot I could catch fire, but the fear of losing him is glacier. Both sensations fight to take hold when he grabs my wrist. The one with the cuff.

With slow, deliberate intent, Griffin removes the band, tosses it on the ground. His stare challenges me to rebuke the action. Or maybe that's not the challenge. For as long as I've known him, experienced his myriad moods, I can't read him right now.

"I don't want to play games," he says, his lips inches from mine. His hot breath melting the icy fear working its way into every cell. "Right here, right now, in this room, we are equals. I don't command you. I won't demand anything but honesty. And I promise to give it in return."

His hips press against mine, the hard bulge in his pants unmistakable.

I'm already hard. Have been since I opened the door, first put my eyes on him. That's what he does to me. But now, with him so close, us touching, him asking me to be myself, my need for him borders on painful.

I force my lips to move, mouth to work. "Okay."

"Are you in love with me?"

I stare into his deep brown eyes. Eyes that have trained me, watched me become the man I am. A man who, even if it costs me everything, owes him the truth.

"Yes."

Griffin's lips crash against mine. One hand grabs my hip, the other the back of my neck.

Stunned, all I can do is kiss him back, hard, desperate, the same way I feel.

Before my body has a chance to respond, and my hands to do a bit of roaming of their own, Griffin pulls away.

We're both breathing hard when he rests his forehead against mine.

"It's a bad idea, you falling for me." He nips at my lower lip with his teeth.

"It was a bad idea to train with you, too. Guess I'm terrible at making decisions. While I'm on a roll, I want to make another one. Be my first."

Griffin's body freezes, not even one muscle twitch. "Aiden, I—"

"It should be you," I cut him off. "It's yours. It's always been yours. No matter what...I mean, even if we don't—you know, after tonight, if this ends, I want to remember losing my virginity to you. Please, Griffin. Mr. Hart. Sir. After living a life full of regrets, don't make me have one more."

When Griffin puts his lips on mine, I know he's making me a promise. A promise that giving myself to him is one regret I won't have.

With our tongues intertwined, Griffin leads me to the bed. When we fall, his weight pushes into me in all the right places. Unfortunately, also in the wrong places.

Bruised ribs scream for relief, my jaw begging not to be worked so hard. Griffin's reaction is immediate. Using his arms, he pushes off me, his kisses turning light.

"I'm sorry." He tries to get up.

I grab a fistful of his sweater, pull him back down on top of me, deepen our kiss.

"I'm the one who'll be sorry if you stop." I bite his earlobe, lick the side of his neck then show him mine, my sign of submission.

He bites my flesh, licks away the ache. "I don't want to hurt you, Aiden. Don't want to be too rough."

"You forget." I slide my hand down his chest, across his stomach, underneath the band of his slacks, cup him through his underwear. "You trained me to withstand copious amounts of abuse and pain. What good is all that training if we don't use it?"

I squeeze his shaft, pump up and down a few times. He grinds into me, my ribs warning me about the pressure. I grit my teeth, relish in both how amazing and torturous it feels to have my boss on top of me, about to make me his in the only way that matters.

This time, when he pushes off of me, I let him. Griffin takes his time undressing me, running his hands across my body, worshipping me in a way I never knew I wanted until him. He kisses away the hurt where I've been bruised and cut, nips on the flesh that's unblemished.

I writhe, wanting him to hurry up and take me, wanting him to take every moment of his time. As pieces of my clothes fall to the floor, the pieces that make up me fall together. We fit perfectly. His body, mine. His need to control, my need to be taken.

"I have to get you ready," he says, breaking our kiss.

The look on his face is one of concern, and I think I know why.

Rolling off the bed, I stand and head to the dresser. I open the top drawer, pull out a small bottle of lubricant.

"Here." I toss it to him.

He cocks an eyebrow, and it makes me want to fuck him more.

"What?" I shrug like I'm completely innocent. "You taught me to always be prepared, so I bought that a while back just in case."

He crooks his finger, beckoning me to him. "Come," he commands.

"God, I hope you let me," I mutter, but he hears and chuckles.

When I crawl back onto the bed, he smacks my ass. I jump then moan when he presses his hard cock along my crack.

"Do you feel how hard I am?" he asks, presses into me more.

"Yeah," I answer, breathless, excited, and terrified.

"I can't wait to fuck you, Aiden. To claim your virgin ass, make you mine. Mark you so deep inside, I'll drip out of you for days."

I rut my ass against his length. "Oh, fuck, I want that so much, sir. I want you to take it."

He pops the top on the lube bottle, drizzles a bit on my ass. It's cold, but his fingers quickly warm it up.

A long, low groan escapes my lips when he strokes me, rubs the outer ring of my hole with his fingers. His pressure is gentle, unintrusive. Then he kisses me, shoves his finger inside at the same time, and my moan quickly becomes a mixed cry of pleasure and pain.

He moves inside me the same way his tongue moves against mine. Before long, one finger becomes two. I clench when he gets to three, struggle to relax. My body isn't used to this type of intrusion.

Not that it's all pain. It's so much pleasure. There's so much more that I want from him.

After a few more tries, and a fuck ton of patience, Griffin three fingers slide in easily. "You're ready," he says, and damn. He's never been more right, and more wrong.

Slowly, as if to torture me, Griffin takes his time peeling off his clothes. I can't take my eyes off him. Like the answer key to a final exam, I study the lines of his body, memorize every crease, freckle, and curve.

"You're so fucking gorgeous when you look at me like that," he says, his eyes drinking me in just as much.

"Like what?" I ask.

"Like there isn't anyone in the world you want more than me."

"There isn't," I answer, not even considering the implication, not ashamed to admit the truth.

"Take it." Griffin hands me the bottle of lube. "Make sure I'm good and slick."

I push up to my knees, pop open the top, and squirt the cool gel into my palm, then wrap my hand around his girth. Touching him anytime is hot. Knowing that I'm priming him to fuck me for the first time, to take my virginity, is next level.

When he's fully coated, Griffin guides me with his body back onto the bed. He slides in behind me, in a sort of spooning position. Only, I'm turned so I can see his face, kiss his lips.

He takes my top leg, bends it, and presses it to my chest, opening me up. With one hand on my leg holding it in place, the other at the base of his cock, my boss rubs his head against my primed and ready hole.

"I'm going to go slow. Take it easy for your first time."

"I don't want easy," I argue, pushing back against him.

His thick, engorged head presses against my outer ring. I clench in anticipation, knowing this will hurt, knowing I want this more than I've ever wanted anything.

Letting go of my leg, Griffin grabs my neck, sinks his teeth in the sensitive flesh below my ear. I cry out, writhe with the burn of wanting him, knowing he's denying me.

"You don't think I want to bury my cock in your ass, ride you so hard this bed breaks through the wall? Pound into you until you fucking scream my name?"

I've never heard Griffin sound so off-kilter, out of control.

"I want to, Aiden. I fucking want to. But you know what else I want?" He kisses under my ear where he bit, licks away the hurt.

I shake my head. Definitely whimper.

"I want to keep you safe. I want this to feel good for you. And I want to preserve this tight, virgin asshole of yours for when I use it over and over." He drops his voice so low, it makes him difficult to hear. "There are so many things I want to do with you. I'm determined to see how many of them we get through in one night."

"Oh, fuck," is all I can say to his words, to the sensation of him knocking at my back door. Of me, letting him in.

Lightning dances up my spine, every nerve ending enervated. So very fucking alive. Inch by deliciously agonizing inch, my boss, Griffin Hart, takes my virginity.

Squeezing my eyes tight, I ride the sensation, concentrate on relaxing my hole that wants to tighten around the intrusion. Push it out.

When Griffin bottoms out, he runs his fingers along my jaw, pulls me in for the type of kiss that lets me know I'm his. That he's got me. That he cares about my first time.

Not that I had any doubt.

Releasing a shaky, restrained breath, Griffin asks, "Are you okay?"

My lips move against his when I answer, "No. I'm not fucking okay."

He pulls back, stares at me, studies my face, looking for clues to see what's wrong.

I grin like an idiot, my boss's dick buried deep in my asshole. "I'm whatever the hell is way past okay."

Finding a bit of courage and will of my own, I pull Griffin in for a kiss. This time, when I tell him how I feel with my mouth, he'll have zero doubt that I want him. I'm in love with him. This is perfect.

He moves inside me, slow at first. It hurts, but every time he slides back in all the way, it hurts less, until it doesn't hurt at all. All that's left is everything that feels right.

Griffin picks up his pace. The tip of my cock slaps my stomach every time his hips meet my ass. It feels so fucking good, a fact made evident by the clear string of precum leading from my slit to my abs.

"I'm close," I say, pulling my leg into my chest, opening up even more for him.

Doesn't matter no one's touched my dick, not even me. With the angle, how he's shaped, how he's milking me with every thrust, I'm going to cum for him.

"I'm almost there, Aiden."

He runs his hand down my chest, wraps his fingers tight around my base, making sure I don't go off just yet.

"Fuck!" He curses a few more times, his eyes locking with mine. "Your ass is so tight. It's so good."

"Yeah. It is good," I admit. The kind of good I could get used to.

Griffin doesn't say anything. Doesn't need to. Our bodies are in charge of the conversation now.

Gritting his teeth, jaw clenched tight, Griffin's gentle pace turns brutal. But I can handle it. I want more of it.

His fist around my cock pumps me hard, his hips slapping into me even harder.

The rumbling freight train that is my orgasm speeds down the tracks, engine roaring, whistle screaming. It crashes into me, full force. The unstoppable kind.

With my boss inside me, owning my ass, I cum, the force like a blast from a cannon. The first of my release hits my chin, it's that intense. The rest tries to follow suit.

From neck to navel I'm covered in my own release, my ass flooded with the heat from Griffin.

I don't know how long I go off, how loud I am, or how much either of us cum. All I know is that he's right. He filled me in a way that's going to stick around. Drip slowly out of me. Remind me who this ass belongs to.

Griffin rests his head against mine, both of us fighting for breath.

"Oh my God. Oh my God. Oh my fucking *God*!" Okay, so my vocabulary is severely crippled right now. "That was...I can't..."

Griffin shakes his head. "So don't."

His kiss is slow and sensual, a recount of everything we just did, of everything that led us to this moment.

When he slides out of me, I miss the fullness. Crave his heat. And am grateful for the break.

Starting at my neck, Griffin kisses his way across the landscape of my body. His eyes lock with mine when he reaches my chest.With slow, deliberate movements, he licks every drop of my spent seed from my skin.

The way he looks, the way he's tasting me, makes my cock twinge. Even though I just came, I could go again. For him, again and again and again.

When he reaches my spent, semi-hard erection, he probes my slit with the tip of his tongue, his hand milking anything still left inside. The sensation borders on painful because I'm too sensitive, but it's also amazing.

I want to tell him to stop, scream at him never to stop.

"Wh-What are you doing?" I somehow manage to ask.

He doesn't answer right away. Crawling over the top of me until the full length of his glorious, naked body is pressed against mine, Griffin kisses me, sharing the nectar he just drank.

"What was that for?" I ask when he pulls away.

He runs his thumb along his lower lip then licks it, making sure to waste nothing of my release. Then he just stares, takes me in.

I fidget, not knowing what to do, to say. I'm about to roll off the bed, go to the bathroom and clean up, when he says, "I never want to forget what it tasted like when you lost your virginity to me. Now, we'll both remember."

My muscles seize, my whole body reacting. Desire pools in my gut, an endless well. My hole clenches, pushing some of his spent seed out, wanting more of him inside.

More of him is exactly what he gives me.

Chapter 13

When I wake, Griffin is already gone. His side of the bed cold.

I don't know what I expected after the most amazing night of my life, but I know what I wanted. Another tumble, followed by breakfast, and maybe yet another go.

I get it. He's a busy man, with a company to run. Still, it stings. Though, not as much as my ass. Maybe it's for the best he's giving me time to recuperate.

Rolling over, I plant my face into his pillow, then do the same to the sheets. Griffin's scent lingers, like the ghost of his touch I still feel on my skin. I burn both into my memory so I can revisit last night any time.

After catching a shower, and the tail end of the continental breakfast the hotel offers, I get to work finding an apartment. I'm about an hour in, have contacted at least three potentials, when my phone beeps.

It's a text. From Griffin.

Sir: *I've made the arrangements. You're moving into my condo. Rent a truck if you have to. I want you out of the hotel and in the condo by end of day Sunday. Save your receipts.*

His text leaves zero room for argument or negotiation. I rub at the skin underneath the cuff. It's the first time it's felt like an actual collar. The first time I've chafed under his rule.

His offer is generous. I appreciate it. I do. It's more that, since I'm being forced to be on my own, I want to see if I can make it. See what I'm capable of. I can't do that if I go from one codependent situation to another.

115

I text him back.

Me: *Is that an order?*

Sir: *Does it need to be?*

Sir: *You know how I feel about what happened. Let me take care of this.*

Me: *I appreciate it. I do.*

Sir: *But?*

Me: *But . . .*

I pause, not sure how to word this in a text. Or under any circumstance.

Me: *But I need to start acting like an adult.*

It takes twelve and a half forevers before he texts back.

Sir: *Move in for now. Keep looking for your own place. No reason to settle for something you don't want, or rush into a situation that isn't ideal.*

I grin like an idiot, feeling more adult-like by the second. I just had an actual conversation with my boss, asked for what I wanted, and got it. If that isn't adulting, I don't know what is.

Sir: *Sunday night still stands. I'll leave the keys at the front desk. Don't disappoint me, Mr. Montgomery.*

My cock jumps in my pants. I wasn't even aware I'd gotten a semi just texting with him.

Closing my laptop, I shoot a text to a buddy of mine from school. A friend with a truck.

I don't have too many things in storage, so it shouldn't take more than a few trips to get everything. And it'll save me money. This hotel wasn't cheap.

Doesn't matter my boss told me to save my receipts. I don't want to spend his money just as much as I don't want to spend mine. Plus, adulting. I want to keep that up.

When the phone rings, I answer, thinking it's my buddy with the truck, Scott.

"Hey, Aiden. Long time, no speak."

Geo's cool, mellow voice is on the other end. He sounds about three bong hits to the wind.

"What's up, Geo?" I ask, trying to keep my tone as even as possible. I still haven't forgiven him for the shit he pulled at his house. Honestly, I planned on never talking to him again.

"Say it ain't so." He sings the line from the Weezer song as much as says it. "You really moving into Pop's condo?"

"What are you talking about?" My first reaction to Geo's inquiry is to lie. Avoid conflict.

"Don't play stupid, Aiden. It doesn't suit you."

I don't say anything. Consider hanging up.

"I overheard him talking to the front desk. He gave them your information so they know to expect you. So, you two are, like, a real thing, then? Yeah?"

"I don't want to do this with you, Geo. If you wanna talk, call me when you're sober."

I pull the phone away from my ear, ready to push the red button.

"Wait! Aiden, wait. Truce, okay? Truce."

I put the phone back to my ear.

"I'm calling to apologize for being a dick. I miss having you around. As a friend. So you're dating my dad. Yeah, it's fucking weird. But, man, I've got to get over that. Right?"

"Right." I draw out the word, not sure what Geo's getting at. It can't be this easy with him.

"I know you don't trust me. That's fine. I don't deserve it. Just, give me a chance to earn it back. Make it up to you, you know, that I was a dick. Let me help you move. You cool with that?"

More hands would make light work. And I guess with Scott there, Geo's less likely to act like a world-class douche. Plus, after my night with Griffin, I have to imagine we're moving our relationship to a new level. Getting along with his son is something I'm going to have to do if we plan to have a future.

"All right."

"Yeah? All right?" He chuckles. "Right on."

"I'm still waiting to hear back from a friend. When I know what time, I'll text you the address to my storage unit. We can meet there."

"Cool. I'll catch you later."

"Later." I disconnect the call and ignore the pit in my stomach that's probably there from drinking too much coffee.

Scott texts me back a few hours later, says he can help me on Sunday morning. After letting Geo know the plan, I spend the rest of the day at my storage unit, organizing what I want to take with me to the condo. I manage to get rid of a trash bag worth of stuff, and drop it off at a local thrift store before heading back to the hotel.

The second I fall into bed, I'm hard. The sheets no longer smell like my boss. But the memory of how he touched me, entered me, kissed, licked, and sucked all over my body, is still fresh. My cock remembers how good everything felt, and wants more.

With my boss on my mind, my dick in my hand, I cum hard, and drift off to sleep dreaming about what he'll make me do the next time we're together.

The next day is hot, and one of those rare days in San Diego where the air is as thick and muggy as some of the southern states. Of course it is, because what moving day isn't complete without dehydration and heat stroke. Thank fuck the high rise building—where I'll temporarily live until I get a place of my own—has a large elevator that's relatively fast.

Even with Geo there, it still takes four trips to get everything I need into the condo. For some reason, Scott's truck seems bigger on the outside than it actually is. He jokes it has something to do with the space-time continuum. I'm not a Dr. Who fan, so I don't get it.

On the last run, Geo offers to stay behind. Says he doesn't mind organizing my boxes, putting stuff away. I don't want him going through my things. But there's nothing I have to hide, the biggest secret being I'm dating his dad, which he already knows.

I agree, partly because I'm exhausted, and I don't want to have to unpack all by myself. And partly because I need a break from Geo. While it's true he's been on his best behavior, there's still a shitload of stress riding my shoulders and neck muscles, waiting for him to say the wrong thing. Be a dick. Or come on to me again.

"So, uh, your buddy Geo," Scott starts after we load the last of my stuff into his *short* bed truck.

"What about him?" I ask, braced for...well, I don't know what.

"Are you two, like, a thing?" Scott's hands tighten on the steering wheel, his eyes firm on the road. It's weird for him to ask. As far as Scott knows, I'm straight.

"No!" I say a bit too quick. "Why would you say that?"

He gives me the side-eye. "N-No reason."

I snort. "Scott, you don't ask a question like that for no reason. Besides, I'm not gay."

Bile rises to the back of my throat at the lie, my body rejecting the truth I've worked and *trained* to uncover. Still, it's no one's business. I'm allowed to lie about it, right?

"Oh. Right, yeah. I, uh, wasn't trying to imply anything. Didn't mean to insult you."

What the hell is he talking about? "You didn't insult me. There's nothing wrong with being gay."

Scott blows out a breath of relief, his features relaxing. I hadn't even realized he'd been tense. "Yeah. No, you're right. There isn't."

After a few awkward minutes driving in silence, me trying to figure out what the hell just happened, Scott trying desperately not to look at me, he finally asks, "So, is uh, is Geo single? Seeing anyone?"

Scott's face turns as red as his hair, the splotchy embarrassment crawling down his neck into the collar of his shirt.

I grin, the last few minutes clicking into place.

"As far as I know, he's single. Perpetually single," I emphasize, not wanting Scott to get his hopes up.

"That's fine." He grins back, finally glancing my way. "I'm not looking for anything serious. Just some fun."

"Geo definitely is fun." Scott's gaze becomes curious. "So I've heard." I shrug it off, pretending like I don't have firsthand knowledge of just how good a kisser Geo is. Or how much he's bragged about being good at other things.

Geo has a dick ring. He's shown me. I always took that as a sign he doesn't fuck around in the bedroom. Well, or that he fucks around constantly.

Scott flicks his blinker, exits the freeway into downtown. "And, uh, you're cool with me being interested?"

"I have zero issue with you being gay," I answer, wondering how many of my other friends have hidden their sexuality.

"I'm not gay," Scott amends. "I'm pan. Honestly, if I'm attracted, I'm not picky. Makes life more interesting, you know?"

I don't know, but I nod anyway.

By the time we get back, unload the truck and bring the last few things into the condo, Geo's made amazing progress. The living room is practically set up, and most of the stuff that goes into the bedroom has been arranged neatly in the closet and the dresser belonging to Griffin. The kitchen isn't done, but all the boxes labeled for it are lined against the adjacent wall.

"Wow, Geo," I say as he grabs one of the bags I'm carrying. "Thank you. This place looks great."

"Anything for you, Aiden." He winks my way, then diverts his attention to Scott, who hasn't looked at Geo since we walked in. Hasn't looked at me, either.

"You need a hand, honey?" Geo says to Scott, all sugar sweetness.

Scott blushes, shakes his head, and sets down the boxes in his arms.

Geo glances from Scott to me and back. "Something happen between you two on this last ride?" Geo's tone is light. He's trying to be playful. But I've known him long enough to read the undercurrent of jealousy.

"No!" Scott reacts the same way I had in the truck. "No," he says again, looking more mortified than when Geo called him honey. "It isn't like that." Scott points between him and I. "We're just friends. Aiden's not gay."

Geo cocks a pierced eyebrow in my direction. I shake my head so only he'll notice, beg him with my eyes not to say anything.

The shit-eating grin on his face tells me this was a mistake. Trusting Geo. Letting him help me.

"While Aiden might not be gay, I noticed you didn't say you weren't."

My eyes widen, my shoulders relax. Geo didn't out me. *And*, he's hitting on Scott.

"I didn't." Scott shoves his hands in his pockets, rocks back on his heels. "So..." He runs his hand through his hair, cuts me a look that begs for a few minutes alone with Geo.

"I gotta go to the bathroom," I say, already on the move down the hall.

When I shut the door, I can hear their voices, but not make out what they say. I take my time in the bathroom, grab a washcloth from the cabinet Griffin so nicely stocked. I run it under cold water, sigh when I press it against my asshole, still sore from losing my virginity.

The final time Griffin took me last night, it wasn't gentle. I'd wanted him to go hard. He hadn't disappointed. I'm paying for it now, but it's worth every ache.

When I come out of the bathroom, Geo is standing close to Scott. I think they might be kissing, but when he pulls away, I realize he's just whispered something in Scott's ear. Or shit, I don't know. Maybe they were kissing. None of my business.

Scott clears his throat when I come back into the living room, which is larger than my hotel room was. The condo is nice. Not ostentatious and obscene considering it's just for overnights and entertaining guests. But it's comfortable. Roomy. And I'm sure it's worth a few million dollars.

At least, that's what another condo just sold for in this building a month ago. Thank you, Zillow.

"If we're done, I guess I'll get going?" Scott says as more of a question for Geo than a statement for me.

Geo puts his hand on Scott's chest. He's nicely built, where Geo is more lanky. The tips of Scott's ears redden, but he doesn't step away.

"You have my number," Geo says, leaning in close like he's going to kiss him. "Use it."

Geo lingers for a few moments, and I wonder if it's to see if Scott will make a move. Or if Geo's trying to make me jealous. Neither happen.

"I plan to." Scott pulls away from Geo, gives me a smile, and heads for the door.

"Thanks," I call after him. "I owe you."

"Nah," Scott scoffs, eye-fucking Geo one last time. "I think we're even."

When the door closes, Geo rounds on me, eyes narrowed. "Why didn't you tell me you have such a *hunk* of a friend?"

I cross my arms, my defenses already on high alert. I don't like being alone with Geo.

"I didn't think about it, and I thought you had zero trouble finding men. According to you."

"I don't have trouble," Geo assures me. "And I'm not mad." He approaches, uncrosses my arms. "So knock it off."

I shake out my hands, let out a sigh. "Sorry. It's just...after everything..." I point from him to me. "I didn't know Scott was pan. So I wouldn't have known to tell you about him."

"It's not a big deal. I was just teasing. Listen, in a few weeks, my dad's company is hosting a fundraiser for the surveillance project I told you about. Me and the guys working on it will be offering a demonstration as part of the fundraiser."

"Uh, cool," I say, not sure why he's telling me this.

"I want you to come. Not as my father's personal assistant." He eyes the cuff around my wrist. "But as my guest. I swear I wouldn't have graduated without your help and encouragement. In a really round-a-bout way, this is your success, too. What do you say we put the past behind us? Go back to being friends? I miss us as friends."

His eyes soften and widen. His lips press together. He's giving me his puppy dog face. One I saw plenty after we briefly hooked up, when he'd ask me when we were going to do more together.

Never. The answer was never. Still is.

"Yeah, Geo. Sure. Friends is good."

"You're fidgeting." Geo grabs my hands so I can't clench and unclench my fists. He also stops me from rocking on my heels. I didn't realize I was doing that until now.

"Oh, sorry."

Geo's skin is warm against mine, his scent a bit too strong, like it always is. Like he is.

He steps closer. His thighs rub mine. His breath heats my face.

I back away.

He lets go of my hands. "Don't worry about it. Mind if I use the restroom before I go?" he asks.

It's weird, Geo asking for permission to do something in his father's condo. But I guess it's sorta mine now, which only makes it weirder.

"Sure."

I busy myself in the kitchen, putting away the few things I have, trying not to mix up what's mine and what's Griffin's. Geo takes his time in the bathroom, and I let him. The less interaction, the better. He said he's going after this. I think that's the best idea.

When Geo comes out of the bathroom, I'm by the front door, waiting for him.

"Can't wait for me to leave, can you?" Geo gets right to the point, just like his father. Unlike his father, I don't owe Geo shit. Especially not an explanation.

"I really appreciate your help," I say.

Geo brings me in for a hug. I'm stiff in his arms, not in a good way. I brace, waiting for him to grab my ass. He doesn't, and maybe that's progress.

"It's a fucking hug, Aiden. What? My father won't allow you this?" He pulls back, looks into my eyes.

"This isn't about your father. That's never been the issue between us."

Geo's laugh is short and sharp. "That's not even close to the truth, but okay. Whatever."

He stares into my eyes, looking for what? I don't know. Don't know that I care to figure out Geo's motivations.

"You're really happy, aren't you?" he asks.

"Yeah, I'm happy."

Geo grins, the kind that makes me uneasy. "Then I feel really sorry for you."

He's gone before I can ask him what the hell that means.

Chapter 14

My alarm goes off, reminding me it's Monday morning. Two things are immediately obvious.

One: I'm still sore from the amazing night I spent with Griffin two nights ago—him pushing my boundaries, me realizing just how much I can take. How much more I want to take.

Two: I'm sore because of the move, both physical and mental. Dealing with Geo, with my emotional unease around him, was way more heavy lifting than I was prepared for.

Hitting snooze on my alarm, I convince myself I deserve fifteen more minutes of sleep. The condo isn't far from the office, and I don't need much time to get ready.

I wake to the sound of my phone ringing. It's Griffin's ringtone.

"Sir," I answer, still rubbing sleep from my eyes. Fifteen minutes went by way too fast.

"Do not think, Mr. Montgomery, that just because I took your virginity, spent the night with you, and gave you a condo to live in, that you don't have to report to work on time."

I sit up in my bed—no. Griffin's bed. I don't actually have a bed. That wasn't one of the things my parents threw out on the lawn.

Pulling the phone from my ear, I glance at the time. "*Fuck*!" I'm late. Two hours late.

"I-I'm, uh...I'm sorry, sir. I overslept. My alarm—"

"Are you making excuses, Mr. Montgomery?" His tone is sharp, clipped. I am *so* going to pay for this. Not in a good way.

"No, sir. I'm sorry, sir. I'll be there in thirty minutes."

"You have twenty."

Griffin hangs up. I jump out of bed, hit the shower first, no time to worry about all the ways he'll make me pay. My greedy hole clenches, hoping he'll punish me by ramming my ass until he unloads in it.

That isn't his style, and that punishment would actually reward me, so, definitely not happening. Oh, well. A guy can hope.

Splitting the difference, I barge into my boss's office twenty-five minutes after our phone call. I say barge because, if I'd actually paid attention to the receptionist who tried to stop me, I'd realize Griffin was in a meeting. A meeting that started five minutes ago. A meeting where I was supposed to take notes.

Every eye in the room turns to me. But there are only two I care about.

My mouth goes dry. I lick my lips, thinking somehow that will help. It doesn't.

"I apologize for my tardiness," I say to my boss first, then to the other people in the room, all executives and higher ups in the company.

"It's quite all right, Mr. Montgomery," Griffin says in a way that tells me it isn't all right. "You haven't missed much. Sit." He nods toward the empty chair next to him.

I do as I'm told, fight every impulse I have not to fidget with the cuff around my wrist.

All eyes are still on me. Griffin hasn't resumed the meeting. I have no idea why, even though the sinking feeling in my gut is trying to warn me there's something I'm forgetting.

"Are you ready to take notes, Mr. Montgomery?" Griffin's tone is even. One could say dispassionate. Bored.

I know better. I see the fire he's trying to hide behind the dark depths of his eyes. I hear the inflection that tells me I'm in for a world of hurt, abstinence, and humiliation.

Closing my eyes, I will the burn under my skin to subside. Cold sweat needles the back of my neck, palm of my hands.

Clearing my throat, I stand. "I apologize. I seem to have forgotten my pad and pen. I'll be right back."

I cannot get out of the room fast enough. The receptionist sees the look on my face, cracks an I-told-you-so grin of her own.

"How's it going in there?" she asks, a chuckle in her voice.

"I screwed up," I admit, as if she doesn't know. "Got a pad of paper and a pen I can use?"

She reaches inside one of her many drawers, pulls out a yellow legal pad and two ball point pens. "In case one runs out of ink or breaks," she says at the confused stare I must be giving her. "I'd hate for you to have to come out a second time."

An involuntary shiver runs down my spine. "Thanks," I say, letting the relief of her saving my ass sink into my tone.

"I like you, Aiden. The boss likes you. When he's happy, I'm happy, and the company is happy." She nods at the pad of paper. "So get in there, stop fucking up, and make him happy. Yes?"

She gives me a genuine smile, something she typically reserves for the higher-ups. "And you owe me a coffee."

"I'll buy you lunch," I say over my shoulder, rushing to get back to the meeting.

It's brutal, sitting next to Mr. Hart, knowing I pissed him off. Knowing I'm about to get punished, but having no idea how. Makes it difficult to concentrate on the boring meeting, and I'm not entirely sure my notes are up to par.

When the meeting's over, I wait for the execs to leave, then try to follow them out the door. I need to type up the notes from this meeting, email them to Griffin, and then tend to a few errands I typically do for him on Mondays.

"Stop."

My body obeys before my mind has a chance to even register he's talking to me. It's chaos inside my skull right now as I try and plan the most efficient way to get everything done on time.

Griffin closes his office door. Locks it.

Should the sound of a lock clicking make my dick this hard?

"Where the fuck do you think you're going?"

I hug the notepad to my chest as a type of shield. "To do my job," I answer, surprised my voice works.

"You owe me two hours, Mr. Montgomery."

"I know, sir. I plan on staying late to—"

Griffin Hart, my boss, shuts me up with a kiss. I drop the notepad, grip the front of his suit, rut around with my hips trying to find relief.

"Are you okay?" he says, his lips against mine?

I shake my head. "No. I'm not okay. I'm fucking terrified of what you're going to do to me."

Griffin pulls back, eyes my body like he's checking for something, then grins. "So you weren't late because you were in pain? The move wasn't too much on your injuries?"

He gently touches my ribs, runs the back of his hand across the practically-healed abrasion on my face, palms my ass, rubs his fingers along the outline of my crack.

"No," I admit, wishing I could lie, wishing I could make him take pity on me.

Griffin Hart is not the pitying type.

"I'm late because I accidentally turned off my alarm. Your bed is too good to get out of. Wanted to spend all day in it." I nip at his lower lip. "With you."

He kisses me again, grabs my dick through my trousers, and strokes me. I moan into his mouth, push against his hand harder.

All too quickly, he pulls away, and shit. I'm back to being terrified.

He straightens his suit, pulls on the cuffs of his shirt, all business. "Fear looks good on you, Mr. Montgomery."

"Th-Thank you, sir?" I ask, because I'm not sure that was a compliment.

Griffin checks his wristwatch. "I have another meeting in fifteen," he comments, as if I don't know. But it's a finance meeting, and over a video conference. I typically don't sit in those because they're recorded, and sensitive financial information is discussed.

"Did you want me to take notes?" I ask, not sure where this is going.

"No, Mr. Montgomery. I want you to take off your clothes."

Want and craving flood my bloodstream, mixed with apprehension. It's the middle of the work day. Anyone could come in, could find us doing...whatever he has planned.

"Was I not clear?" He puts his hands in his pockets. Looks as relaxed as if we were on a beach somewhere drinking margaritas.

"Crystal, sir." I still haven't moved.

"Strip," he practically growls. "We don't have much time to get you into position before the meeting starts."

Into position? During the meeting? I open my mouth to question him, maybe even argue that exposing our arrangement at a finance meeting maybe isn't the best way to come out about our relationship.

"The longer you stand there, do nothing, the more I make you wait."

I know exactly what he means. I'd like to cum sometime this month. I've already fucked up enough. I don't need to make my situation any worse.

Moving as fast as my body and fingers can, I undress, fold my clothes into a neat pile, and place them on a chair out of the range of the webcam.

I shiver as the cool office air brushes against my exposed flesh. Even with as nervous and chilled as I am, my cock has no problem standing at full attention. I can't imagine a time when I won't get hard for my boss.

Griffin takes his time admiring my naked body, which makes me fidget. He's the one who said we didn't have much time.

Walking over to his desk, Griffin unlocks the bottom drawer, slides it open, and pulls out a box with another lock on it. Whatever's inside is something he doesn't want nosey employees finding.

Unlocking the box, he flips open the lid and stares at the contents as if he's trying to figure out what it is he wants to take from it.

Finally, he grabs a thick, semi-long, black silicone object with a round disc on the bottom, and a bottle of lube. The level of relief I feel that it isn't a cock cage is a palpable thing.

"Do you know what this is?" he asks, holding up the object.

I shake my head. "No, sir."

"It's a butt plug. You're going to lubricate it, then bend over my desk." Griffin holds out the plug and the lube bottle.

Stepping to him, I take it, hands shaking, and do what he commands. I slick the plug, making sure the lube coats it on all sides, then hand it back to Griffin. Spreading my legs, I place my hands flat on his desk—my face to the computer that will host the video conference in less than ten minutes—and bend over.

My boss drips more lube onto my ass. It slides down my crack as Griffin uses one hand to push my ass cheeks apart, and the other to insert the plug.

I grunt and try not to clench. But I'm still sore from how hard he rode me the other night, and tight because I only just lost my virginity. I'm far from an expert on how to relax.

Thankfully, he doesn't go in far before he pulls it back out. "Fuck. I forget how tight you are. I'm going to have to work you, and if you aren't relaxed enough before the meeting starts, then I guess everyone on the video conference will have to wait, watch me play with your ass, until I can get this in."

He wouldn't.

"Yes, I would," he answers as if I'd spoken aloud.

Spreading my legs wider, I press my chest as far into the desk as it'll go and will the muscles inside my core to soften. Griffin slides the plug further in, circles it around to stretch me.

I release my breath only when he pulls it out. "Breathe," he reminds me as he goes at me again, this time almost getting it in all the way.

"So close," he encourages, pulling it out again. My hands grip the side of his desk, my forehead pressing into the cool wood.

This time, when he pushes the butt plug inside me, it's all the way. Full and stretched, Griffin smacks my ass. I jump, but don't dare change positions. Don't dare cry out.

Grabbing a handful of my hair, Griffin pulls me to standing. I have to clench hard to keep the plug from sliding out.

"You like having things in your ass, don't you?" He's using the tone that tells me we're in our roles. Him the master. Me the submissive.

"Yes, sir."

"And you like having things in your mouth?"

"Yes, sir."

He rubs the flesh he just smacked, taking away the sting. "Then I'll make you a deal. For the next hour, I have to be on a conference call. You're going to be under my desk for all of it, sucking my cock, licking my balls. Your mouth better not leave my body, or I'll cage you for a week. Understand?"

"Yes, sir."

"If you're good, do what I say, pleasure me under my desk during the meeting, keep the plug in the whole time, then when the meeting is over, I'll fuck your ass, cum deep inside you. Is that what you want?"

My dick pulses and swirls in the air. It's hard. Painfully hard. The precum dripping from my slit all the answer he needs.

"Yeah. That's what you want." He swipes at the precum with his fingers. Puts his fingers to my lips until I open my mouth, my tongue licking off my own excitement.

His computer chimes, alerting him that the conference call is about to start.

I squeeze underneath his desk. It's tight, and I have to sit at an awkward angle, but for my boss, I'll do what I have to to please him.

It's only an hour, I tell myself. How hard can it be?

Ten minutes in, and already, my body screams for me to change position. My jaw aches from opening for Griffin's thick, magnificent cock. When I move my legs and shift my grip on him, needle-pricks dance up my arms, across my calves.

I can't cry out, no matter how much I want to. The execs on the call would hear me, and I don't want Griffin to have to explain why his assistant is under his desk, blowing him.

At the same time I'm willing my body to calm the hell down, the plug slips from my ass. I twist my arm behind me, catch it with my hand. I might've saved the plug, but my lips pull away from Griffin's cock.

Shit. I'm like a human pretzel down here. Maybe I should've just let him lock me up.

Pushing the plug back in, I sit on my legs, use the heel of my foot to keep it in place. Griffin's hand appears out of nowhere, his fingers tangling in my hair. He pulls my face into his crotch, taps the side of my head to let me know that was my one warning, all while not losing a beat during the meeting.

How he can focus on number crunching while getting his dick sucked is beyond me. When Griffin's mouth is on my body, anywhere on my body, all I can concentrate on is him.

I lose track of time after that. When my muscles beg for a change in position, I ignore them. When my jaw finally burns so bad my vision blurs, I switch to licking his balls. I use my hand to keep pace on his cock.

The first time my boss cums is a total surprise. He gives zero indication. No change in breathing or speech patterns. No discernable tell. It's why my face catches the brunt of it, the thick liquid dripping off my chin onto my chest. I clean myself and him as best I can, but I'm still a mess.

The second time he cums, I learn his tell. It's subtle, especially since he's talking at the time. But I know that when his thighs harden into stones, and his shoes make a slight creaking noise from his toes curling under, I need to be ready to drink him down.

The hot, sticky release from my boss fills my mouth, slides down my throat. This time, I catch all of him. His musky taste explodes across my tongue, and I lap at his slit, making sure to milk his shaft for every drop.

He's sensitive after the second orgasm, so I back off. Give his balls more attention. It takes him longer to get hard afterward, but he does. I'm wondering how fast I can make him give me a third load when he ends the meeting and disconnects the call.

Before I know what's happening, his fingers tangle in my hair, and he yanks me from beneath his desk.

I stumble, my body numb from being in one position for so long. My muscles burn when my blood tries to reoxygenate them. The plug slips from my ass, thunks against the ground. I reach for it.

"Leave it." Griffin's voice is little more than a growl.

With his grip on the back of my head, he slams me into his desk, kicks my legs apart. My hard cock rubs against the ridge of the desk. I cry out, both in torment and ecstatic anticipation.

I want him. And I want him to take me rough.

The sound of his buckle rattling, his zipper being yanked down, causes my asshole to pucker.

"Are you ready to get fucked, Mr. Montgomery?" My boss rubs the tip of his cock along my ass crack, pops open the bottle of lube. "To pay me for the hour you still owe for being late?"

I push my hips back. It's as much to rub harder against him as it is to make space for my own hard length squished against the desk.

"Yes, sir. I'm sorry I was late, sir. You're right to punish me. I promise not to do it again."

He uses the head of his cock to rub more lube on my hole. "And if you do?"

"Then you can punish me just like this, every time."

Setting down the bottle next to my head, Griffin places one hand at the base of his dick, the other on my ass cheek. Without warning, and without taking his time, my boss slams into me, balls deep, filling my tight ex-virgin hole that he's already claimed.

I cry out, then remember to keep it down. We're in his office, building full of his employees, and my boss is ramming my ass.

With his hand on the side of my face, Griffin pushes me into the desk, uses the leverage to hold me in place as he jackhammers away. The force of him makes our skin slap together, makes the wooden desk beneath us groan. The slick, wet noises from my hole as it grips my boss's cock take me to the edge.

I rut against the desk, try and find some relief, some way to escape the rising tide deep in my gut.

"I'm not going to last, sir."

"Me, either," he grunts, his whole body shaking with the effort of fucking me hard. "Your tight ass is too good, Aiden."

At the sound of my name on his lips, I lose it. Warmth splashes across my belly, coats his desk in my spent seed. Ramming deep into me, Griffin's dick jerks, pulls against my internal walls. I squeeze him tight, milk him with my ass, not wanting him to pull out.

When he does, I miss the fullness of him. Love the way he drips from me, coats my thighs, runs down my legs. I'm thankful there's a desk underneath me, holding me up, because I can't catch my breath, and my body is going to need a moment to properly function.

Too impatient to wait for me to stand on my own, Griffin pulls me up by my shoulders, turns me to face him, and kisses me so deep, I forget to breathe.

When he releases me, it's too soon, but I know what he's about to make me do. I made a mess. I have to clean it up.

Shoving my face into the mess, Griffin watches as I lick my spent seed off his desk.

The phone on his desk beeps. It's his receptionist.

"Sorry to bother you, Mr. Hart. I noticed you were off your conference call and wanted to get you this information right away."

Griffin hits the button to answer while holding my head firmly in place, the message clear. Don't stop cleaning. "Go ahead."

"Your son called. Said he needs to reschedule today's meeting."

"That's fine," Griffin answers, not taking his eyes off me. "I'll take an extended lunch. Forward my calls to my cell."

"Yes, Mr. Hart."

The line goes silent. I slurp up the last of my cum off the wood.

This time, when my boss pulls me to standing, he doesn't kiss me. "Clean up." He nods toward the private bathroom inside his huge office. "Be quick, and when you finish, you and I are going to have a lunch meeting at the condo, where we'll discuss your performance. I'm not done punishing you, Mr. Montgomery."

"Good," I say, putting all of my need for him into one word.

When we leave his office, I try not to look anyone in the eyes. They'll know what we've done if I do, I'm convinced of it.

Griffin and I don't make it back to the office after lunch. In fact, the for rest of the week, Mr. Hart has to extend every lunch. Even cancel a few meetings.

It makes me feel special, cared for, that he's willing to break the rules a little to spend time with me. Make me a priority. I'm not used to how that feels, and it makes me love him more.

And even though I'm still looking for my own place, I love that we have a place together, a sanctuary that's just ours. I'm in no rush for anything to change.

Life is just too perfect.

Chapter 15

"Tell me again what my son said when he invited you to this fundraiser."

Griffin stands behind me, his stern reflection a distraction as I try and knot my tie. He's already impeccably dressed, and looks like the billion dollars he's worth. Probably worth. I don't actually know for sure, and it's never mattered.

To prove that point, when he offered to buy me something to wear, I said no. I didn't want to spend his money. I'm already living with him. He's doing plenty.

The downside is that the thrift stores I typically frequent didn't have anything that fit. Or matched. I spent way too long piecemealing this outfit together. And I still look like crap.

Whatever. I'm clearly not an investor, anyway. I'm going to support Geo, not model for the cover of a fashion magazine.

As if that were even possible.

"He said he wanted to go back to being just friends. Told me I helped him get through college, that he wants to share his success with me. Honestly, Grif, he probably just wants to rub it in my face how smart he is."

I huff out a breath, ready to tear off my tie and burn it on the stove. I've never had this much trouble. But with how bad my hands are shaking, the butterflies in my stomach morphing into angry piranhas, I'm surprised I haven't had a nervous breakdown.

The thought of being in a room full of rich, powerful men isn't what scares me. It's the fear of being in the same room with both Griffin and Geo. I don't want to be responsible for family drama. Especially not with so many eyes on us. Doesn't help that the fundraiser is being held at Griffin's...house? Estate? Whatever.

In addition, I found my own place. Just happened yesterday. Got a call back on an apartment I really wanted, located close to work, but was told there was a lot of competition. I'd written it off. Forgot about it. Hadn't told Griffin. I'll have to tell him tonight.

Griffin steps in behind me, the front of him pressing against every available inch of my backside.

Taking the tie from me, he lifts an eyebrow as he stares at me through the mirror. "Grif?" he husks in my ear, his eyes never leaving mine as he ties the perfect fucking knot.

I turn in his arms, rest my palms against his chest. "Too much?" I ask, giving him the same look he's giving me.

His hands find my hips, and he pushes me back against the counter. "Careful, Mr. Montgomery. Or I'll rip these clothes off you, fuck you until you can't walk, then make you wear *my clothes* to the fundraiser. Or nothing but a cage and a collar."

My dick was already hard at the word *careful*. By the time he finishes, I'm ready to let him do anything he wants to me.

"Okay," my mouth says, the heat in my blood all too ready to comply.

Griffin cups my dick through my pants, rubs me in the way that drives me wild. My hips buck against his hand, and I'm about ready to tear off my own clothes, when he pulls away.

I groan. Want so fucking bad to complain. To beg him to at least jack me off. I don't. Training with my boss has taught me better than that.

His teeth find my earlobe, his lips brush against the sensitive flesh. "I want you to be thinking about me tonight. No matter who you choose to socialize with, I want your mind on me."

"You don't have to tease me to get that," I offer, hoping he'll give me relief. "I'm already consumed by you."

"True." He rubs me some more, my hard length becoming almost painful. My boxer briefs absorbing the wet leaking from my slit. "But I want you to be ready, and more than willing, when I find you later tonight, take you into my home office—for old time's sake—bend you over my desk, and claim your ass.

He drops something into the pocket of my suit jacket. It's small, but heavy. Reaching in, my fingers graze familiar plastic, cool to the touch. It's a tiny bottle of lube.

My dick jumps in my pants, my head leaking more precum. "Why do we have to wait?" I know I'm begging, that I sound pathetic. Don't. Fucking. Care. "Fuck me now. Right here. *And* you can take me later."

Griffin's lips find mine. He pulls me in for the kind of wicked kiss that promises so much pleasure, but not without a price.

His voice is barely a whisper when he says, "You know why we have to wait." He grabs a handful of my ass, pulls me tight against him. "I enjoy watching you squirm."

I don't enjoy squirming, and for the next two hours, I can't get comfortable. Never mind that I'm sweating in this suit, or that I keep screwing up the names of the important people I've met, or that social gatherings in general make me anxious. All of that pales in comparison to the deep seeded ache creeping through my system like poisonous vines, the epicenter my groin.

I love that Griffin knows exactly how to torture me for maximum effect. And I hate him for it.

When Geo asks me what's up, I tell him I'm nervous about telling his dad I'm moving out. For some reason, that makes Geo happier than I've seen him in a long time.

"Trouble in paradise?" Geo asks, his black leather coat with a ruffled tail making his Goth-Punk formal outfit look sharp. The pale powder covering his face, and his smoky eye, would be overkill for anyone else. On Geo, it fits perfectly.

"No." I straighten the arms on my third-hand suit jacket, try my damndest not to feel like a slob. "Nothing like that."

His grin falters, replaced by a blank mask. On him, with the makeup and clothes, it looks terrifying.

"Grif—uh, your dad has been very generous, giving me a place to stay. The arrangement was always temporary. I told him I'd planned on finding a new place. I don't want to take advantage."

Geo studies me for a moment, some kind of champagne drink in his hand. "You aren't the one who's taking advantage, Aiden."

I open my mouth to ask him what the hell, when Griffin interrupts us. "Mind if I steal Mr. Montgomery away for a few moments?"

My boss's hand rests gently on my lower back, already guiding me away from his son. Geo watches, an unreadable expression on his face. "Sure. But the demonstration will start soon, and I don't want either of you to miss it." He pouts to really sell that he wants us here.

I don't buy it. Geo's been busy all night, schmoozing with money, and the men and women who can give it to him. Geo's charming, when properly motivated. It doesn't take much to motivate him. Booze and gay porn come to mind.

Griffin reaches out, places his hand on Geo's face. For the briefest moment, I see the young boy behind the makeup and black. The kid who craves his father's attention and approval.

I don't know what it was like for Geo, growing up with such a powerful father. I can't imagine they spent much time together. Building an empire the way Griffin has must've taken up all of his available time, leaving little for Geo.

But what the hell do I know? I'm not an expert, and I could be wrong. I don't think I am, and the way Geo leans into his father's touch tells me I'm not.

"I'm proud of you, son. Wouldn't miss the demonstration for the world."

"Good," Geo says, pulling back. "I'm sure it's one you won't forget."

Griffin lets his hand fall to his side. When it does, his arm grazes against my pocket. The one with the lube bottle in it.

"Mr. Montgomery and I have some business to discuss. Don't worry, it'll be quick. We'll be back before anything starts."

I shoot my boss a look that begs him not to hit on me in front of Geo, but the smolder in his dark eyes makes me forget whatever the hell I was thinking. My eyes widen when they meet his, my dick instantly hard, not that I haven't been sporting a semi all night. I'm pretty damn sure my face, neck, and the tips of my ears turn a splotchy shade of pink.

"Sure. Whatever." Geo turns his back to talk to someone else. Someone with money.

Without another look my way, Griffin cuts through the crowd, makes his way toward the kitchen, to the stairs leading to his office. He stops a few times to talk to people he knows. I stand behind him, smile, and remain quiet.

It's less out of respect, more because my dick is so hard it hurts. I'm afraid if I open my mouth, say anything, it'll be to beg Griffin to fuck me right here and now, audience be damned.

I'm through the office door first, my eyes landing on his desk. How in the hell does something so mundane stir emotions that are completely erotic?

My answer stands behind me, issuing commands. "On your knees, Mr. Montgomery."

I hit them, glance up at him through my lashes, and open my mouth, ready. He unzips his dress pants, cock springing free. The instant it's out, I'm on it.

Taking him in as far as I can, I hold him in my mouth, his tip down my throat, and move my tongue. He moans, his fingers tangling in my gelled hair, messing up the style. When I pull back, I lick up his shaft, swirl my tongue around his head, lap at the excitement beading in his slit.

"Oh, God, Aiden. Your mouth feels amazing."

It should. I've spent months learning exactly how my boss likes his dick to be sucked.

With one hand on his sac, the other around his base, I get to work bringing him to the edge. Like they always do when he's close, his thigh muscles harden, his grip tightens. Instead of unloading in my mouth, he pulls out before I can make him go off.

"No," he pants, his eyes hooded at he stares down at me on my knees. "Not yet. I want to save this for your ass."

I clench at his words, and rise when he pulls me up. He holds out his hand. I place the small bottle of lube into it, then start to undo my pants.

"Stop."

I freeze, wait for his next command.

Setting the lube down on his desk, he brings his hands to my buckle. Slowly, with patient practice, Griffin Hart takes his time undoing my pants. Unmaking me.

By the time they fall to the floor, my underwear with them, I'm shaking. I'm so on edge, the slightest touch is enough.

Griffin leans his forehead against mine, our heated breath mixing together. "You are so fucking beautiful when you're this ready for me."

"I am ready, sir. Please, *please* take me."

Pushing me back against the desk, Griffin coaxes me onto it, facing him. He brings one of my feet to the desk, the other to his shoulder, and encourages me to lean back. I comply, eager to do what he says. I let him guide me, give him what he wants. Let him give me what I want.

My dick slaps against my stomach when he pulls me toward him, my ass hanging off the edge. Dripping lube down his entire erect length, he rubs it in, coats himself, then slicks my asshole with what's left.

"I'm going to fuck you hard," he husks, then bites my neck. I cry out, enjoy his lips and teeth on me. "Can you handle that?"

"Yes," I practically beg. "Yes. Go hard. Make me sore. Mark me as yours."

Griffin closes his eyes for a second, sucks in a sharp breath. "Mine," he finally says, his voice low, controlled, even if the look behind his eyes is wild.

Pressing into me, my boss slides the head of his cock against my opening, then pushes inside. It burns, but I've learned how to adjust quickly.

He goes slow, giving me time to stretch, enjoying how tight I am. When he's all the way in, he holds himself there, pushes me so I'm leaning back farther, which changes the angle, then enters me even further.

I look into his eyes. Take in the curve of his lips. The crease in his brow as he concentrates on filling me. He's in deep. And I'm in deep with him.

With the same slow, gentle patience Griffin used to enter me, he pulls out. His breath catches when he says my name, "Aiden."

My entire body shudders with just that one word. With the sound of me on his lips. And then, he makes me shudder for other reasons.

Working his hips, using my angle for leverage, Griffin gives me everything I begged for. He goes hard, like he promised, my ass and thighs taking the brunt of the force. I grip the edge of his desk to hold myself in place, bend my legs as much as I can so that every thrust is a little bit deeper. So that, when he fills me with his cum, it'll stay inside me for days.

It isn't long before the muscles in my stomach tighten. The rushing pressure thrums through my bloodstream, builds up between my legs. I open my mouth to beg him to let me cum, to beg him to cum with me.

"I'm there," he says before I have the chance, his words wound as tight as I am. Almost as tight as his hand around my cock.

He pumps me hard, pumps into me even harder. Not for the first time, I pray his office is soundproof as I shout out the pure bliss of letting go. Of having him let go with me.

If I could bottle this sensation, I'd be the billionaire.

I clean up using the private bath off his home office, not for the first time, noting how both his offices have private baths. I'm grateful they do.

When I step out of the bathroom, Griffin is there, waiting. His clothes and hair are impeccable. No one would know he just fucked me like a beast. I, on the other hand, look like I've been ridden hard.

And I was.

I've done my best with my hair and clothes. If anyone notices...I don't know. Whatever. They won't. And who cares?

"What's on your mind?" Griffin's cologne envelops me as he steps close.

I stare at my shoes, the floor, anywhere but his eyes. "It's nothing. I'll tell you later. Or never." I mutter the last, but I'm sure he hears.

Placing his fingers underneath my chin, he lifts until I'm facing him. "Tell me what."

"I found an apartment," I blurt, deciding it's better to rip off the Band-Aid than slowly peel it away. "It'll be ready next week. I-I, uh, I'll move over the weekend. Won't take any time off. I just...I mean, I thought I should tell you."

Silence stretches between us, but the look on Griffin's face doesn't change. If he's pissed I'm leaving, or hurt I didn't tell him sooner, or happy I'm finally getting the fuck out, he doesn't show it.

After what feels like an eternity—which is probably only really thirty seconds—all the self-doubt and negative talk starts chattering away inside my head.

We've been happy these past few weeks. Why am I screwing it up?

He's so angry right now, he can't even speak.

He's thinking of fifty ways to break it off with me.

This is it. He's done using me. He's taken what he wanted. This is where I get kicked to the curb.

"Move in with me."

Those four words rock my world harder than all my other bullshit thoughts combined.

His hand finds my cheek, his thumb rubbing against my skin in the way I've grown used to. "I don't mean the condo. I mean here. In this house. Date me, Aiden. Publically. I don't want to hide us anymore."

Now I'm the one who's silent. I don't know what to say, how to respond. He wants me to *move in with him*. Be his, officially.

"Wh-What, uh..." I lick my lips, a nervous habit, something I do too often around him. "What about my job?"

Griffin laughs. I immediately feel like I've said something stupid.

"I ask you to move in with me. Be mine. And you're worried about your job?"

Seemed like a reasonable question to me. "Yeah."

He kisses me suddenly, in a way that removes any doubt. In a way that says we both know I'm already his.

When he pulls away, he runs his fingers down my forearm, across my wrist. "You're fired, Mr. Montgomery."

I frown as he removes the cuff and pockets it.

"Fired, sir? From what? My job as your assistant, or as your sub?"

"Your job." He grins as he taps his pocket. "This is still yours, if you want it."

"I do," I say, practically talking over him.

"*But*, I don't want you wearing it when you give me your decision. I need you to know you have an equal say in this. I'm asking for a lot, Aiden. I'm asking you to be my partner. My lover. Mine. And I'm asking you not to hide it."

My mouth opens. Closes. Opens again. Nothing comes out, partly because I'm too in love with him to speak, and partly because all the reasons I wanted to move out of his condo still exist.

I need to practice being my own person. See what kind of man I am without the influence of my father.

Then again, Griffin Hart has shown me exactly what type of man I can be.

"You don't have to give me an answer right now," Griffin says. "If you need more time, take it."

He steps in closer, puts his hands on my hips, and runs his nose up the side of my neck. I moan, unable to help it. "Just, don't keep me waiting too long. You know how impatient I get when you make me wait."

How in the hell is it possible I'm hard again, when I just went off so completely?

"If I'm going to be your partner, I need to help pay rent and bills." I tilt my head to the side, give my boss—uh, my *ex*-boss—more access to all the spots that make me melt under his firm, attentive caress.

"Okay," Griffin mutters against my skin.

"I can't do that if I don't have a job. And I clearly can't work for you."

He bites my earlobe, licks away the sting. "No, you can't. I'll give you a recommendation. Put in a good word for you with friends of mine who run their own companies."

Sliding my fingers across his shoulders, I find my way to the nape of his neck and tug on his hair. "Good. Because it's important to me that I work. That I contribute to whatever we create between us. That I'm not a kept man."

Griffin pulls back, pins me with his heated gaze. "I want to keep you. Put you under lock and key."

"I want you to cuff me," I assure him. "In the bedroom, you can lock me up any way you want. But in every other aspect of my life, I need a win. Need to feel like I can do this."

"I understand, Aiden. Whatever you need to make this work, I'm willing," he says, and I believe him.

Griffin didn't start out as who he is. He built the man in front of me from the ground up. From nothing. From rejection, and the pain and damage caused by his own father.

"Okay," I say, wanting so bad for his mouth to be on me again.

"Okay?" He runs the pad of his thumb across my lips. "Does this mean you're saying yes?" he asks, as if there was ever a possibility I wouldn't.

"Yes. It means I'm saying yes."

Chapter 16

I make it back upstairs just in time for Geo's presentation. Griffin and I had left his office at different times so it wouldn't look suspicious. I hated it, told him I couldn't wait until we no longer have to hide our relationship.

When Geo catches my eyes, I wave. He looks pissed, and I can't figure out why. I'm here, ready for his big moment. Does he still hate that me and his dad are together? I thought he got over that.

He stalks over to me as the other three members of his collaboration and design team talk with potential investors. I always thought Geo worked with a group of guys, because he always called them "the guys." But two of the co-inventors of the surveillance technology are female.

I don't know why I'm surprised. I don't think Geo gives much credence to gender. Or to the idea that sexuality is a defined thing.

"My father really should be more gentle with you." Geo's fingers find my tie. He straightens out the knot and tightens it, then fluffs out the wrinkles in my jacket. When he runs his hands through my hair, failing as miserably as I did to do something with it, he says, "You look like a fuckin' wreck."

My face heats, partly because he's right, and I know it. And partly because talking about the sex I just had with his dad is the last thing I want to do.

"Sorry?" I say, not really sure why I'm apologizing. Maybe old habit.

"Don't worry." The infamous Geo grin is back, replacing the bitter twist of his features. "Everyone will be looking at me, not you. It's a good thing I'm so damn handsome."

He winks, pats my shoulder, then joins his co-inventors at the front of the room. They stand next to a large screen with computers and other equipment set up nearby.

"I think it's time we get started." Geo claps his hands together, getting everyone's attention.

I find Griffin across the room. My face heats again, this time for a completely different reason. His lips twitch, his dark eyes glinting with mischief, with the knowledge only the two of us have.

I said yes. After tonight, I'm going to be Griffin Hart's official boyfriend.

The screen lights up as Geo gives his well practiced speech. That he's a smooth-talking charmer was obvious the moment I first met him at school. That he's Griffin Hart's son has never been more obvious than it is now. Geo makes the technical jargon of the project easy to understand, interesting to follow.

"We now bring you to the best part of our presentation," Lanying, one of the co-creators, explains as Geo sits next to the equipment, starts typing furiously on his laptop. "The part you've all been waiting for."

The large screen lights up, images flashing across it, first with their logo, then with some technical aspects.

"All of the images we're about to show were gained with permission from several cooperating companies and individuals," Lanying explains. "Each have asked us to hack past their firewalls to see what we could obtain."

Geo stops typing, glances up at me, and smiles. I smile back, my stomach twisting painfully with that look. I don't know why I should feel so nervous for Geo. Maybe it's because I want him to succeed. Despite everything, we're friends, and he's very talented. I hope he gets everything he's asking for.

"We hope you enjoy," Geo announces to the room. So, why does it feel like he's talking only to me?

He hits a button on his computer, and all eyes go to the screen.

Dockets of financial information, security plans, and private emails dance across the screen. Some members in the crowd grumble, presumably because it was their company Geo hacked, for lack of a better term.

Next, the screen shows videos from private security cameras. More grumbling, and the shuffle of nervous feet make me think Geo's doing a good job. That the product does everything he brags it does, and more.

"I have another meeting in fifteen."

Griffin's voice sounds from the screen. My gaze shifts from the man in real life to the man about to make me pay for being late.

"Did you want me to take notes?"

"No, Mr. Montgomery. I want you to take off your clothes."

The room is silent. Every eye that was on Geo and his crew is now on Mr. Hart. And me.

"Was I not clear?" Video Griffin shoves his hands into his pockets.

"Crystal, sir."

"Strip." The commanding growl in his voice rumbles over the speakers, vibrates every molecule of air in the room.

None of that air makes its way into my lungs. I can't breathe. Can't think. Can't do anything as the blood in my veins turns to ice, freezing me in place.

My brain screams at me to do something. It wants to rationalize that Geo wouldn't do this to me. To his father. But he is doing it. He's ruining both of us.

"Do you know what this is? It's a butt plug. You're going to lubricate it, then bend over my desk."

All I can do is watch as I follow his commands, die a little inside when he slides the plug into my ass. My face contorts with the kind of private pleasure I reserve only for Griffin, now on display for the entire room.

"Geo? What the fuck is the meaning of this?" the real Griffin, the *now* Griffin, asks. No, not asks. Yells.

"You like having things in your ass, don't you?"

The recording of Griffin is so good, so real, I almost answer.

"Yes, sir."

"And you like having things in your mouth?"

"Yes, sir."

"Then I'll make you a deal. For the next hour, I have to be on a conference call. You're going to be under my desk for all of it, sucking my cock, licking my balls."

There's commotion on the other side of the room. I don't look, can't take my eyes off the screen, off the movie of my life falling apart.

"If you're good, do what I say, pleasure me under my desk during the meeting, then when the meeting is over, I'll fuck your ass, cum deep inside you. Is that what you want?"

It isn't what I want. Right now, all I want is to die. Is to run. Is to never have to face anyone in this room ever again, including Griffin Hart.

"Yeah. That's what you want."

The video shifts, this time showing images of the long lunches Griffin and I took away from work. Lunches that we spent at the condo. In our bedroom.

Geo wanting to help me move in makes perfect sense now. He didn't want to help. He wanted to plant recording devices. Wanted to expose our private life.

The final bit of video shows the session Griffin and I just had in his office downstairs. When he cums, and I cum with him, my stomach twists so violently, I think I'm going to vomit.

I have to go. Need to get out of here. Need to run.

The video feed finally cuts off. The silence that had so completely enveloped the room explodes, destroying the moments I'd shared with my boss. Destroying everything.

I'm shaking so hard, I have no idea how I move. Later, I'll probably be grateful my body has its own ideas about what to do, my mind completely checked out.

I stumble toward the front door. Hands grab my arms. Voices try and talk to me, try and stop me. I push past, push everyone away.

The doorknob is cool to the touch, the design leaving indentations in my skin from gripping it so hard. The night air is still. Calm. Peaceful. It beckons me. Calls me to it. Promises me things that I'll never have again.

"Aiden. Wait!" someone calls out.

Not someone. My boss. Ex-boss. Ex-lover. Ex-dom. Ex-everything.

I don't wait. I can't. If I stay, I'll hurt someone. Do something I regret.

I laugh at that thought. At how stupid it is.

My feet hit the stairs leading away from the door. From the house that was going to be my new home. From the life I just said yes to.

As soon as my feet hit pavement, I run. I run, and run, and don't stop until I think my lungs might explode. Until my calves burn. Until I can finally release the scream trapped inside my throat.

Once I do, I drop to my knees, empty the contents of my stomach on the side of the road the same way I empty my heart.

Chapter 17

I call Lily, then turn my phone off.

I don't know why I call her, but for some reason, I know I can trust her to be here for me. To not judge. To help me because I need her to.

She comes to get me, doesn't say a word until I'm ready to talk. It's a long time before I'm ready to talk.

"Thank you," is the only thing I manage to say before tears make it impossible to do anything but let everything out.

She lets me tell her what happened at my own pace, takes me back to her house so we can relax. Her father offers me the couch to sleep on for the night. I take it, and also take the old t-shirt and shorts he offers.

I throw my suit into the trash, shoes and all, and promise Mr. McCabe I'll replace the clothes he lent me. He tells me not to worry about it. They don't fit him anymore anyway.

Lily and I are still up when the sun rises. I tell her everything. Absolutely everything. She makes us coffee, flicks on the television when we need a break.

My face pops up on the screen, along with Griffin Hart's. Our affair, and the trouble it's caused him, is already splashed all over the news outlets, and it isn't even eight in the morning. Our sex scandal is followed up by the arrest of one Geo Hart. Turns out, the FBI doesn't take kindly to espionage, network hacking, and embezzlement. He'd been using his invention to cause a lot more harm than good.

Lily turns off the TV, scowls at it, then rubs my shoulders. I'm numb, too broken to feel just how completely broken I am.

It's three days before I get off the McCabe's couch. Three days before I turn on my phone, dare to look at social media. As expected, I have over a hundred texts and messages, most of them from Griffin. I delete every single one without reading or listening to them, then wipe his contact information from my phone.

On Facebook alone, I easily have a thousand notifications. I glance at only the highlights. Most of the people in my timeline are supportive. Outraged something like this happened to me. That I was taken advantage of at work, made to serve such a slave-driver of a boss. Many of those same people let me know they still love me, doesn't matter I'm gay.

Fuck. I didn't even think about that. I don't get to choose how I want to come out. *If* I want to come out. Social media and cable news networks have done that for me.

What I don't see on my phone, don't expect to see, are any messages from my parents. But someone does share a YouTube video to my timeline. A reporter was stupid enough to interview my mother and father about their son's role in the downfall of business mogul, Griffin Hart.

I get a good laugh at the look on my father's face, and feel nothing but sorry for my parents when my mother shoves the cameraman and says, "We don't have a son. He's dead to us."

The people in the comments section calling out my parents for being bigoted fucks don't realize I'd long ago died in their eyes. Me being gay is simply another nail in an otherwise heavily metalled coffin.

The first time I leave Lily's house is a nightmare. I need clothes, having left everything I own at either Griffin's condo, or the storage unit. Honestly, I don't want any of it. I'd rather leave it all behind, just like I plan on leaving my life behind.

The only thing from my past I do go and get is my car. It's painful, stepping into the condo after everything that happened. But I need to leave Griffin his keys. Need him to know I'm done.

After leaving the condo, I pull into the parking lot of the local thrift store. I'm not there more than twenty minutes when news vans pull up. Reporters jockey for position, lob questions at me like darts, hoping one of them will hit bullseye. I don't play their game, ignore them as best I can, pay for my shit, and get the hell out.

It's difficult not running over people standing in front of your car, pounding on your windows. I mean, it's tempting. Seriously. How dare these assholes harass me at the worst time in my life? If I want to talk, I will. They don't get to bully me into doing an interview. I'm past being bullied.

The next day, my phone rings so much, I think about drowning it in the sink. The first seven calls are from Griffin. I ignore them. The next is from some lawyer's office. I answer that one.

They want to represent me. Offer to sue the hell out of Griffin Hart and his company for what he did to me. I kindly explain that he didn't do anything. That I chose to be in a relationship with him. And to leave me the fuck alone.

The next call I get from a lawyer's office has me ready to bitch them out. Then I realize they represent Griffin and the company, and want to offer me a settlement in exchange for a signed NDA and the promise not to sue at a future date.

I tell them I don't need a lawyer of my own. Tell them Griffin Hart did nothing wrong. Tell them he shouldn't lose his company over this.

Nothing I say seems to matter. They still insist on paying me. Eventually, I relent. I need the money, and it's a lot of money.

I also get a message from my father's cousin, someone I didn't even know existed. Said she had a falling out with my father many years back. Says they never saw eye-to-eye about social issues. Susan, is her name, and she offers me a job as an office manager. In Oregon.

I kiss Lily on the cheek, hug Mr. and Mrs. McCabe, and hand them a check for rent before getting into my car and driving to Oregon, four weeks after I first crashed on their couch. I can't leave California, and all the mistakes I've made, fast enough.

It takes six months before I stop obsessing over everything that went wrong with me and Griffin as I lie in bed, unable to sleep. Another several before my dreams stop featuring my greatest humiliation, my biggest regret.

As it turns out, I'm pretty damn good at this office manager gig. I'm super organized with a hyper sense toward detail, thanks to all the training I'd done with Griffin, not just in the bedroom.

One year after I ran away from my old life, I start my own consulting business. With Susan's help, I pick up a few clients. Word of mouth spreads like an epidemic after that. I take my hobby-turned-business and make it a full time, legit thing. Even hire a part-time employee. An assistant. A *female* assistant.

It's also a year before I even think about dating again. It sucks, because everyone I meet, I compare to Griffin Hart. And the truth is, no one compares to Griffin Hart.

Only once do I get far enough to try and have sex with someone who isn't *him*. It doesn't go well. He isn't gentle. He doesn't know my body, care about my pleasure, the way Griffin used to. It's fine. It is. I don't crave it, not like I did when we were together.

The thing I miss more than the amazing sex, more than anything, is the intimacy. The way Griffin would test my boundaries, push against them to see if they'd move. He was somewhere safe, someone I could explore with. I'll probably never find that again. With the way I left him, maybe I don't deserve to.

Two years after California, and a year into my business, I receive a letter offering to buy my company. They want to pay me two million dollars, and hire me on to consult and train new staff.

I stare at the letter, not sure if it's a joke. A call a few days later assures me it isn't a joke. The buyer wants a meeting with me to discuss the terms of our agreement. I say yes, because two million dollars is a lot of damn money.

Determined to make sure my part-time employee gets hired on full-time, I head into the meeting, dressed to negotiate. My suit is a far cry from the piecemeal one I'd worn the night...

I shake my head, clear the nasty thoughts. Doesn't matter it's been over two years. Wouldn't matter if it were twenty. I'll never forget that night. Never forget what was taken from me, what I walked away from.

I've lost track of the number of times I've picked up my phone, stared at it, willed Griffin Hart to call me out of the blue. Or, maybe, for me to dial his number. Neither happened.

Griffin stopped trying to call me before I left California. And now, too much time has passed where I've done nothing. Let my silence say everything my mouth, and heart, were too afraid to.

I can't imagine what he must think of me. I don't want to know. It can't be anything kind.

Straightening out my jacket, smoothing down my hair, I open the glass door and greet the receptionist. She leads me to a private office, no windows, and asks me to take a seat. When she offers me some water, I decline. Hopefully, this won't take long, not that I have a bustling social life waiting for me.

What I have is a cat and a one bedroom apartment. It isn't much, my life. But it's mine. In a way, it's what I've always wanted, always needed to prove. That I could do this, be a man, on my own. If this deal goes through, I'd say I've accomplished that goal.

It's a win that feels good. Bittersweet, but good.

As I wait, I let my eyes wander around the office. It's sparsely decorated and furnished. A few black and white poster-sized photos of mountains, the chair I'm in, and a desk.

But, fuck. That desk, though. A tingle I feel when I think of only one thing, of only one man, starts deep in my core. It isn't the same desk. Can't be.

Stepping closer, I study the lacquered wood, notice scratch marks that look too familiar. Leaning down until my face almost touches it, I inhale. It smells just like I remember, and I should know. I spent plenty of time face down on this desk.

This exact desk.

The office door opens and closes. I start to stand, to turn and face the party interested in buying my business. But I know better, the desk the dead giveaway. This isn't a business meeting. This is something else.

Right on cue, a voice straight from my past ghosts into my present, making my heart stop.

"I'm glad you could come, Mr. Montgomery."

Chapter 18

My body freezes, my blood icing the same way it did that night. Fear courses through me, igniting my fight or flight instinct. But something stronger conflagrates within me, begs me to stay, craves the man standing before me.

The urge to hit my knees, bow my head, wait for his instruction, is so strong, my legs wobble. I have to fight to stay upright.

It's in this moment I know, without a shred of doubt, cutting him out of my life was a mistake. The worst mistake I've ever made.

Maybe forever passes between us, and maybe I don't miss a beat when I say, "Sir?"

Flames roll through me, burning just underneath my skin. How can one simple word unmake me, set me right back to where I used to be? Where I should be? Should've been this whole time?

Griffin Hart makes a noise in the back of his throat. Through sheer will, I force the cells in my body to cooperate, make my motor neurons respond.

Shaking off my statue-like pose, I push away from the chair I'd been sitting in and turn to face my one-time boss, lover, confidant. He's as breathtakingly stunning as the day I first met him. More stunning.

His gray hair is longer in the front than I've ever seen him wear it. And the impeccably styled suits I'm used to have been replaced with business casual meant for comfort. Still, his linen pants probably cost more than what I used to make in a week.

"You look good," he says, shoving his hands into his pockets, looking a hundred times more relaxed than I feel. "Oregon's treated you well?"

My mind runs over the million things I want to say to him. The scenarios I've played out as fantasies, of what I'd do if Griffin Hart ever waltzed back into my life. None of them happen. None of them come close to preparing me for the riptide emotions the drag me under the ocean of denial I've been swimming in. Drowning in.

I love this man. No matter how much time passes, that will never change. My chest aches at that realization, and I know I let Geo, and my own cowardice, ruin something most people only dream about finding.

Griffin's brow furrows. His luscious lips press thin. His eyes soften. "Aiden?"

The sound of my name on his lips breaks me. Wait. Who the hell am I kidding? Leaving him broke me. Him being here now, it does something else.

Tears prick my eyes, but I'm determined not to cry in front of him. "I'm sorry," are the only two words I manage before my throat closes around the rest.

Griffin pulls his hand from his pocket, runs it through his hair, exhales a breath as if he's as nervous as I am.

"Sorry about what? About the past two years, or that I'm here now?" His tone is hard. Even. Measured. It isn't cruel, and for that, I'm grateful. No, it's more like he's trying to protect himself. From what? I don't know.

I have to imagine a man like Griffin Hart knows how to move on. So why does it seem like this is as hard for him as it is for me? He can't still care about me. Not after what I've done.

Clearing my throat to dislodge the knot, I square my shoulders, straighten my tie. Doesn't matter that, inside, I'm dying. This is a business deal. For the next hour, I can pretend this is nothing more. I know how to endure torture. Pain. Humiliation. Griffin and his son have taught me well.

"Neither," I say, offering nothing more. "Our past isn't why we're here. I'm surprised to see you, actually. I did my research. As far as I can tell, you don't work for this company."

Mr. Hart studies me for a moment. His eyes roam over my body, linger on certain areas he knows intimately. I suppress the shiver of desire slithering down my spine, coiling deep in my gut. Deny the impulse to drop to my knees, beg him to forgive me, beg him to punish me.

For two years, I've craved the kind of control Griffin offered. No one's come close to it, the attempts laughable. Or tragic, depending on the perspective and mood. Yet, here he is, less than ten feet away. He might as well be ten thousand miles for all the distance between us.

"I don't work here. A friend of mine owns the company."

"Of course he does," I mutter, not surprised that, even after the fallout, Griffin still has friends in high places.

"I asked him to reach out to you as a favor," he continues, as if I said nothing.

Annoyance mixed with disappointment makes me clench my jaw. "So, I'm not here to make a business deal?"

"You are. If you're willing to deal with me." Griffin flicks his hand toward the desk, inviting me to sit. When I don't take the invitation, he grins.

Fuck! My ex-boss is breathtaking, his face lighting up the way it used to in private moments. And I hate he still owns me, even if I can never admit it.

"You want to buy my consulting firm? Hire me on to work for you?" Because working for Griffin Hart ended so spectacularly last time.

"Yes, and no." Griffin takes the chair on the opposite side of the desk. Steepling his hands, he rests his chin against his fingers. "I don't want to hire you. I want to partner with you. Equal footing. Fifty-fifty. I see the man you've become. I'm impressed at what you've built. On your own." His lips tilt in a sad frown. "Isn't that what you wanted?"

"It is. Was. Thank you, sir." I close my eyes, try to remember to loosen my jaw, and will my blood pressure back into an acceptable range. Even after two years, calling him sir is still a habit, taking a compliment from him still just as hard.

If my slip up bothers him, Griffin doesn't show it.

"I'm building a startup, one based in internet and financial security. With your talent, and organization skills, I think we can make this a multi-million dollar venture. Might only take a few years. Probably less."

"Partner?" I ask, because I've never seen myself on the same level as Griffin Hart. "You want me to be your partner?"

Too late, I realize how that sounds. But I'm not about to take it back.

Griffin doesn't miss a beat. "I want nothing more, Mr. Montgomery. Nothing."

He pauses, letting his words sink in to all the places I shut off, closed down. Thought would never see the light of day again.

"After what happened with Geo," he continues, pointing once more to the chair, "I saw an opportunity."

I cross my arms, continue to refuse to sit. I don't know why I'm being stubborn. Maybe to prove a point. My way of saying he no longer controls me, even if every single fiber of me wants him to.

"An opportunity is one way to look at it. Glad to see the most traumatic and humiliating day of my life wasn't completely for nothing."

Griffin's features soften. He breaks eye contact first, as if he isn't strong enough to face me, to face what happened. My heart breaks at the gesture, because I know what happened caused him pain. It still does.

Releasing a deep breath, and the tension in my shoulders, I take the seat offered, place my hands on the same desk I've gripped and scratched. "I apologize. That wasn't fair."

"No, it was." His dark, knowing eyes find mine, intense, focused. It was easier when he wasn't staring. "I deserve that. I knew Geo had been an issue for you, and I didn't protect you."

"He's your son," I say, keeping as much of my emotion from my voice as I can. "I understand the choice."

"I chose you, Aiden."

My eyes widen. My chest warms at those words.

"I'd told Geo he needed to move out, told him I was going to ask you to move in. I just didn't think...I shouldn't have given him as much access as I did. I failed my son, in so many ways. His retaliation was aimed at me, but hurt you, and I allowed that to happen."

I scoff, shake my head. "I'm pretty sure Geo's retaliation was aimed at us both. Your son never liked hearing the word no, and I was never going to give him what he wanted."

"Geo's in federal prison," Griffin says, his brow furrowing. "Did you know that?"

I do know.

I know about everything that's happened to him and his son ever since that night. I know Griffin was threatened with legal action if he didn't step down as CEO. He was publicly shamed and humiliated, his name synonymous with sexual harassment. I know he had to sell his house and most of his assets, that he was forced to walk away from his old life in a similar manner as I had.

"I'm sorry. That must've been difficult for you," I say, instead of all the other crap.

He gives me a sad smile. Behind his eyes is a bone weary tiredness mixed with deep sadness. They're both looks I've perfected. Can easily recognize in others.

"What was difficult was losing you." Griffin reaches into his pocket, removes something small, metallic.

A key.

I swear my dick jumps at the memory of being locked up. Denied pleasure. Only to be given something better.

I lick my lips, a nervous habit I had when we were together. "Wh-What's that for?"

"You left everything behind, and I didn't have the heart to throw anything out. I moved your belongings to a storage unit not far from here." He shoves the key closer to me. "It's yours, if you want it."

Slowly, I reach for the key, my hand shaking. "You did that? For me?"

Palming the tiny metal object representing such a huge gesture, I hold it to my chest, the ridged edges cutting into my skin. This is about more than access to my stuff. It's Griffin's way of offering me the pieces of my past that were good. If I want them.

"I'd do anything for you, Aiden," he says so low I almost don't hear. He scrubs his hand over his face, shifts his gaze to the desk that holds so many memories. "Anything but let you go."

Opening the top desk drawer, Griffin pulls out a small, square box and places it between us.

"This is yours." He gestures to the box. "It will always be yours, nobody else's, whether you choose to wear it or not. Either way, I'm done with it."

Done? Does he mean done with me? Or...?

I slide the box closer, open the lid. Inside is my bracelet.

This time, when tears come to my eyes, I can't stop them.

"I love you," he says, and could he stop destroying me? "I already loved you when you told me you felt the same, maybe a bit before. I didn't expect to find you, didn't expect to fall. And I sure in fuck can't accept I've lost you."

My breath catches in my throat as I stare at the bracelet through a bleary sheen of wet.

"Please, tell me I haven't lost you."

Silence envelops me, the stillness a threshold between annihilation and salvation. My vision tunnels until all I can see is the box. All I can hear is the furious rhythm of my pounding heart. All I can smell is the lacquered desk, reminding my body of all the reasons I've never been able to put Griffin Hart out of my mind. Out of my soul.

Griffin stands, comes around to my side of the desk, kneels at my feet.

Griffin Fucking Hart kneels at *my* feet.

"Aiden, please," he begs, his voice breaking on my name. "I could survive anything, fight my way back from anywhere. I don't want to do any of that if you aren't by my side. And if you hate me, never want to see me again, never want me to contact you, then man up and tell me. I need to hear it from your lips, because your silence has been torture. It's been worse than knowing one way or another."

With Herculean effort, I tear my eyes away from the cuff, cut my gaze to the man on his knees in front of me. The man I love more than my next breath. The man I will always love.

I open my mouth to say...what? There aren't words for how I feel, what I need. Simply saying "I love you" back seems cheap, somehow.

Instead of trying to fit something as immense and impossible to describe as what Griffin Hart means to me into something as defined and limited as language, I reach for the bracelet.

The metal is cool to the touch, the weight of it familiar in my palm. I unscrew it, wrap it around my wrist, and hold my arm out for Griffin so he can clasp it. Collar me. Claim me. Make me his.

He stares at the bracelet, then at me. Seconds tick by. Seconds wasted, where his mouth isn't on mine, his flesh not against my flesh. We've wasted enough time.

Grabbing a fistful of his shirt, I pull him close and shove my wrist into his open hand. When I speak, my voice is practically a growl. "Lock it."

He does. And as he does, his hands shake.

When it's done, when I'm his again, I use the handful of shirt I grabbed and drag his mouth to mine. The feel of him, the taste of him, is like coming home.

I know I'm finally where I belong.

Griffin moans into my mouth, takes the kiss deeper than I have the guts to. We're still in an office building, in the middle of the day, where anyone could walk in on us. He doesn't seem to care. Right now, I don't, either.

The whole world has seen us do worse, the video Geo made probably still circulating the internet. And I'm past the place where I feel the need to hide my sexuality.

Pulling me from my chair, Griffin pushes me until I'm sitting on the desk. I open my legs. Griffin kicks the chair away, slides between them. I grab two handfuls of his ass. It's just as firm, just as enticing, as the last time I was with him.

Cupping my jaw, Griffin pulls away. "I'm renting an apartment nearby. Come home with me," he insists as he peppers kisses along my neck. "There are so many things I want to do with you, but not here."

I squeeze him with my thighs, pull him in closer using his shirt. "If you think taking me to your apartment, tying me up, and fucking me senseless will make me sell you my business to become your partner..."

I bite his lower lip, then suck on it, as my palm skims down his stomach to the bulge in the front of his pants. "...then you're absolutely right."

Griffin growls when he drags me to my feet. "You don't have to make this decision now. I'll take you to my place and fuck you either way." He grins, and hell. Seeing him happy, knowing I put that smile there, is like a kick to the chest that sends a consuming flame through my bloodstream.

It's a sensation I hope never fades.

Reaching up to touch his face, I run my fingertips across his cheek, into his hair, then down the back of his neck. "The answer is yes."

His hands find my hips. "Yes?"

"I want to be your partner. In all the ways," I say. "On one condition."

"Anything," he says against my ear as he bites the lobe gently.

"Anything?" I tease. "Seems your negotiating skills could use some work."

He cups my ass, pushes his knee between my legs. "My negotiating skills are just fine."

I groan, close my eyes, enjoy the sensation of how perfectly he knows my body. Knows precisely how to touch me.

"Okay, then. My demand is that we hire on my assistant full time, all the benefits."

Griffin releases me, steps back, and glares. "Assistant? He any good?"

Now it's my turn to grin. "*She's* amazing."

Griffin nods. "Deal. Now for my demands."

Sliding his hand down my arm, Griffin grabs my wrist, runs his fingers underneath the cuff.

I shiver, my dick hard, ready. For him. "Anything," I husk as his breath mixes with mine, our mouths close.

"Anything?" he throws back at me, mocking my tone from before.

"Anything, *sir*."

His grip on my bracelet tightens, his dark eyes boring into mine, seeing all the way into my damn soul. Damned because it'll never belong to anyone but him.

The next time Griffin Hart opens his mouth, it changes my world. Changes everything.

"Marry me."

Epilogue

"Stop," Griffin's dom voice, the one I've come to love and respect, commands from over my shoulder.

I stare at him in the mirror, the lights around it giving his dark irises haloes.

Stepping behind me, Griffin brings his fingers to my tie, expertly knotting it.

"How do you *do* that?" I ask when he finishes, the knot so perfect he could give training classes to tailors.

"Practice," he husks into my ear, then runs his lips up my neck.

"Isn't it bad luck to see the groom before the wedding?" I tease as I tilt my head, give him more access to my skin.

Griffin's arms go around my waist. He presses into me, his steel length rubbing against my ass cheek.

"Only for the bride." He slides his palms down my inner thighs, taunting me. As if I'm not already as hard as he is just by looking at him.

Dressed to kill, he's easily the most gorgeous man at our wedding. Hell, the state. The entire planet.

He moves his hips against me the same way he did last night. I hate that we're both fully dressed. Something we could remedy, though I can't imagine our guests would appreciate that.

"Clearly, I'm not a bride," he says, as if he needs words to make the point. He doesn't.

"If you don't stop grinding on me, we're going to be late for our own wedding. And I'll probably destroy that tux."

"Destroy it." He strokes my dick through my pants, driving me wild. "As long as I get to destroy something else, I don't care." He moves his hand from my front and slides it across my crack.

I rut against his hand, pushing into him hard. "Fuck this," I growl and start to unzip my pants. Screw everyone else. They can wait.

A loud knock sounds at the door. "Aiden, it's time. Are you ready?"

Lily's voice cools the raging inferno making lava of my blood. Maybe, just maybe, I'll get through the next few hours without jumping my soon-to-be-husband.

Soon-to-be-husband. Damn. It still doesn't seem real.

When Griffin asked me to marry him, I was stunned. But I knew the answer before he even asked. He wanted to elope right away. I made him wait until we got the new company going, could prove it was a viable business.

I figured trying to manage a marriage and a new startup was a recipe for disaster. Plus, it gave us time to figure things out, work our way through the damage we'd done to each other. Heal, so we could start again. Better this time. Stronger. Equal.

I rub my wrist out of habit, even though I'm not wearing the cuff.

"I think he's ready," Griffin answers for me, and screw him and the look on his face.

Leaning down, Griffin kisses me, deep, hard, and too short. "See you at the altar," he whispers, then he's gone.

Lily steps into the bathroom, taking his place. She tangles her fingers with mine, smiles up at me. She looks stunning, and happy. I'm happy for her.

Because of what she's done for me, how she stuck by my side when I really needed her, I've grown to consider her as a sister. We may not have married each other, but I don't think we could've ever been closer than we are now.

"I'm proud of you." She fusses with my hair. I swat her away because it's pointless. She outmaneuvers me, determined to tame my wild locks.

"Yeah?" I squeeze her fingers tangled with mine when she finishes.

"Yeah. You've come so far, fought for so much. You deserve this, Aiden. Deserve to be so happy your cheeks hurt. If it weren't for you, I wouldn't have known it was okay to follow my heart. To be the person I was meant to be. You gave me that."

I pull her in for a hug, kiss her forehead. "Thank you for being here today. For walking me down the aisle. There's no one I'd rather it be."

She gives me a sad smile, knows better than to mention my parents.

By the time we reach the main room, and Lily and I step into the aisle leading to the altar, my stomach is no longer a stomach but an angry nest of hornets stinging my nerve endings. The old me surfaces for a moment as every eye turns our way. My mind plays out the events of *that night*, of my learned pattern of not being good enough. Of not being man enough.

Then I catch Griffin's eye, the look of deep love in his features, and all of that bullshit self-talk goes away. So does everyone else, until it's just me and him, and less than a hundred feet to our forever.

The actual ceremony goes by in a blur. More than once, I worry my heart might actually burst. I've never felt this warm and tingly. This cherished. This lucky. This in love.

When it comes to the part to exchange our vows, I say, "I do," before the officiant gives me my lines. Everyone laughs, because it's funny. I think I might vomit.

"Do you have the ring?" the officiant asks.

Both Griffin and I reach into our pockets at the same time, each pulling out identical cuff bracelets, his matching the one he bought me all those years ago. Feels like a lifetime ago.

This time, when he locks mine, his hands are steady. When I lock his, mine shake. He takes my hands in his, holds them until I take a deep breath, calm myself as much as I can.

"I am yours as much as you've been mine since the day I first trained you." He flicks his wrist, his bracelet sliding along his skin. "Now, the world will know it."

When we're told to seal our union with a kiss, Griffin cradles my face, devours my mouth like a drowning man taking his first gulp of air. Catcalls and wolf whistles sound from the audience, but I don't care.

The reception flies by. I'm so high on endorphins that I never want this day to end. But then I remember what I get at the end of the day, and it can't go by fast enough.

I let Griffin carry me over the threshold of the home we bought and made ours, together. I do what he says, follow his directions, when he commands me to stand still, not say a word.

He takes his sweet, torturous time just staring at me, com-miting to memory the way I look. The way I smell. The way the electric buzz of our love permeates the air between us.

Over and over again, I have to fight the impulse to fidget, especially when he starts to undress me. He's a cruel, sadistic bastard in the languid way he removes my clothes, keeping his fully on. In the way he *doesn't* touch what I so badly want him to. Which is basically anywhere. Everywhere.

By the time I'm naked, my dick is painfully hard and practi-cally dripping. Griffin drops to one knee, flicks his tongue out, catches my taste. I almost fucking lose it, break my role, grab his hair, beg him to suck me, then fuck me.

I don't, because if there's anything I've learned in life, it's that I'm stronger than I think I am. I'm more comfortable in my body than I've ever been, and I'm fully aware of my bound-aries. Plus, I like when Griffin tests just how flexible they are.

Fuck, is he testing them now.

Somehow, by some miracle, I don't move, don't make a sound, as he swirls his tongue around my swollen head. As he laps at my dripping pleasure.

Standing, Griffin puts his mouth on mine. The taste of him and me mix together into a bit of an addiction I've developed.

Removing his mouth from mine, Griffin leaves the room without a word. A few moments later, he returns with rope, a chair, a very familiar butt plug, and some lube. After slicking my hole, then slicking the plug, Griffin instructs me to sit on top of it, on the chair.

I slide down slowly, relishing in the way the bulbous shape stretches me. The way it fills me, puts pressure on my prostate and the muscles lining my inner walls.

Balls full, dick hard, ass stretched, Griffin takes in the sight of me ready for him. "You are so fucking beautiful, and I am so in love with you," he whispers as he ties my hands behind my back, my feet to the chair.

I can't move, don't even bother trying. No point. Griffin knows what he's doing, in all the ways that matter.

"Are you ready?" he asks once he's done tying me up, admiring his handy work.

I don't know what he has in mind, but that doesn't stop me from nodding my head.

His lips twist with the kind of wicked grin that tells me I'm in for something special. "Good. I'm ready, too."

Griffin starts at his tie, slowly undoing it first. Then he removes his tux jacket, shirt, and finally his pants. His boxer briefs strain to hold him in, the fabric pressed to the limit by the iron rod I wish he'd spear me with.

But when he drops his underwear, my eyes widen, and a pulse of craving makes my dick jump. He's wearing a harness. An ass plug harness held together by a ring around his cock.

I make a sound in the back of my throat, fighting back the words, "Oh my *God*." He told me not to talk, not to make a sound. And I don't want to ruin whatever inspired him to wear that.

He cuts me a hard look. I do my best to school my features in place, lasso my wild, out of control desire.

"Do you like it?" he asks, and is he for fucking real?

I nod once, proud of myself for not shouting, "*Fuck, yes!*"

"I wore it all day," he confesses as he drops to his knees in front of me. "Wanted to be ready for tonight. For what I plan to do with you."

Without warning, Griffin dips his head, wraps his lips around my cock, and sucks me in the way only he can.

I close my eyes, force my lungs to fill with air, and squirm around the fullness of the plug in my ass, only adding to the pleasure overload. My need for my new husband, coupled with my desire to please him, to hold out, is so strong, I think I might hyperventilate.

He works me with his hot mouth, his expert tongue, to the point of madness. Every muscle in my body fights against the cresting wave of the best orgasm of my life. And because he knows me so well, Griffin pulls off my cock before I go off, denying me what I want more than almost anything.

I cry out, because I can't help it, and he's already punishing me anyway. What more could he do?

He slaps my balls, not hard enough to really hurt me, but just hard enough to make it sting, bring me back from the edge. It's his way of letting me know he's still in control. That there are consequences for not doing what I've been trained to do.

Standing, Griffin undoes the buckles and straps holding his harness in place. I watch his every move, my eyes glued to the man before me. The man I love with everything I am, everything I'll ever be.

When he steps out of the harness, he slicks my cock with more lube, then slicks his asshole. I don't understand why until he slides over my legs, sits in my lap, and angles my dick for his hole.

Face-to-face, our breath mingling, I look into Griffin's deep brown eyes as he slides me inside him, his warm flesh sheathing me all the way. I've never been with any man this way. Another first. And hell, I did *not* know what I was missing.

I moan, and fuck it. He can make me pay all he wants. It will be worth it. Everything has been worth it for this moment, right now, with him.

When I bottom out inside him, he claims my mouth with his. As his tongue moves inside me, he glides his hips up and down, rides me to the same rhythm. His cock strokes my stomach with the motion, and I know I won't last long.

"Grif—" I try and warn him, but then he squeezes my cock with his ass, and the only noises I'm capable of making aren't words.

"I know you're close, *husband.*" He draws out the word. It's a word that could make me lose it even if we weren't doing this. "I'm going to let you cum inside me, fill my ass, claim it the way I've claimed yours so many times."

He picks up the pace, and it's all I can do to hold out.

"We're in this together, Aiden." He holds up his wrist, the one with the cuff on it. "This is my way of showing it."

Rising up, he slams down on my cock. Hard. Something inside me breaks apart, breaks open. I clench...hell, *everywhere*, the plug in my ass and the ropes around my arms and legs the only things anchoring me.

Griffin's pace doesn't stop, the muscles deep inside him milking my orgasm, drawing it out until I beg him to stop. Until every nerve ending burns with the relief of release, leaving me barely more than a raw, frayed thing.

"I love you," his lips say against mine, his breath hot against my cheeks.

I can't see, my vision blurry from whatever high being this in love and satisfied brings. "I love you, too. So much," I think I say. I'm not sure. I don't even know my own name right now.

My breathing hasn't calmed when my husband slides off my spent cock. I miss being inside him, definitely want to do that again. But I want him inside me more, want to bring him as much pleasure as he's brought me.

Starting with my legs, Griffin unties the ropes, then massages the sensitive flesh. When he drags me to my feet, I sway, my muscles too relaxed to properly function. The plug falls out, and he tells me to leave it.

Good, because I'm not sure I could pick it up, anyway. I'm not even sure how he's going to take me. I'm basically useless right now.

Using his body, and his powerful presence, he guides me to the bed. Our bed. He turns me on my side, spoons me, the same position as when he took my virginity.

When he slides inside me, my body begs for a break. Begs him to give me more.

I don't know how long we make love, kiss like there's no one in the world but us. And I sure in hell don't know how he lasts so long. What I do know is that he gets me hard again, works me into a frenzy. I beg him to go harder, to just fucking take me, wreck me.

I don't care how sore I'll be later, not when every ounce of available concentration is focused on how amazing Griffin feels right now.

How complete I finally am.

How much I'm going to enjoy being trained to be his for the rest of our forever.

• • • •

THIS IS THE END OF Aiden and Griffin's story. I hope you fell in love with them almost as hard as I did writing them, as hard as they did for each other.

Did you enjoy reading this story? Want to see more like this? If so, please **leave a review**. One or two sentences is enough, and reviews support your favorite authors, help our works get seen by more people. What you think matters.

• • • •

JOIN CHARLOTTE STORM'S VIP mailing list to get an **exclusive M/F BDSM download**, and all the latest news about new releases, giveaways, and freebies!

https://www.subscribepage.com/CharlotteStorm

Follow Charlotte Storm's Amazon Author Page:

https://www.amazon.com/Charlotte-Storm/e/B07B7QMR4G

Listen to all of Charlotte Storm's Audio Books Here:

https://www.audible.com/author/Charlotte-Storm/B07B7QMR4G

Other Works By Charlotte Storm

The Secret: https://www.amazon.com/dp/B07C9CM88Y

What We Hide (Sequel to The Secret): https://www.amazon.com/dp/B07C79HYB1

Secrets We Hide (2-part FFM Bisexual Manage): https://www.amazon.com/dp/B07FGW4Z82

NOW ON AUDIBLE: https://www.audible.com/pd/B07FTNF387/?source_code=AUDFPWS0223189MWT-BK-ACX0-122879&ref=acx_bty_BK_ACX0_122879_rh_us

• • • •

TRAINED BY MY WIFE'S Brother: https://www.amazon.com/dp/B07BT8G96D

Trained By The Boss: https://www.amazon.com/dp/B07DKRDNZ9

• • • •

WAKE FOR ME (AN EROTIC thriller) ~ https://www.amazon.com/dp/1981021817

NOW ON AUDIBLE!: https://www.audible.com/pd/B07DRPZ5W4/?source_code=AUDFPWS0223189MWT-BK-ACX0-119246&ref=acx_bty_BK_ACX0_119246_rh_us

• • • •

THE WEDDING TRAIN (A MMFMMMM Cuckold):

Behind The Red Curtain At Nightingale's Presents . . .

B ehind The Red Curtain 4-story Bundle (with never before published story!): https://www.amazon.com/dp/B07C7QTVKJ

Fae's First Time: https://www.amazon.com/First-Behind-Curtain-Nightingales-Presents-ebook/dp/B07B3SCNK2/

Submission Of Aphrodite

https://www.amazon.com/Submission-Aphrodite-Curtain-Nightingales-Presents-ebook/dp/B07B943WSM

Humiliating The Demon's Mate: https://www.amazon.com/dp/B07BHZHNML

Cheaters Always Finish Series

Perfect 10 ~ Cheaters Always Finish Collection (with two never before published stories!): https://www.amazon.com/dp/B07D5QVFSG

Cheater's Reunion: https://www.amazon.com/dp/B07B89WT1D/

NOW ON AUDIBLE: https://www.audible.com/pd/Cheaters-Reunion-A-High-School-Reunion-Revenge-Cheat-Cheaters-Always-Finish-Audiobook/B07HM95RZ7

Cheating With Him: https://www.amazon.com/Cheating-Him-erotic-Cheaters-Always-ebook/dp/B07B93YWYJ

NOW ON AUDIBLE: https://www.audible.com/pd/Cheating-with-Him-M-M-Straight-to-Gay-First-Time-Audiobook/B07HNDRGFN

Cheating With His Brother: https://www.amazon.com/dp/B07BBPZLQM

NOW ON AUDIBLE: https://www.audible.com/pd/Cheating-with-His-Brother-Audiobook/B07H4YJ827

Cheater Next Door Part One: https://www.amazon.com/dp/B07BLK3MT1

Cheater Next Door Part Two: https://www.amazon.com/dp/B07BLJZNV9

Cheater's Bundle: Kiara & Kevin: https://www.amazon.com/dp/B07BSKZC1V

NOW ON AUDIBLE: https://www.audible.com/pd/Cheaters-Bundle-Kiara-Kevin-Audiobook/B07HKQHQVK

Cheater In Aisle 7: https://www.amazon.com/dp/B07BVQ9HF9

Cheating With My Best Friend's Dad: https://www.amazon.com/dp/B07BZ21LML

NOW ON AUDIBLE: https://www.audible.com/pd/B07GQ4PXNF/?source_code=AUDFPWS0223189MWT-BK-ACX0-125650&ref=acx_bty_BK_ACX0_125650_rh_us

Cheater Below Deck: https://www.amazon.com/dp/B07CVGBV61

The Bored Housewives Sub Club

Borrowing My Best Friend's Stepson Parts 1 & 2: https://www.amazon.com/dp/B07H718LCR/

Riding the Bull: https://www.amazon.com/dp/B07HH4PBPP

Writing As C.C. Wylde

Fight Twice For Me ~ Two Stepbrothers Are Better Than One: https://entangledpublishing.com/fight-twice-for-me-two-stepbrothers-are-better-than-one.html